The Devils of Los Angeles
A Crime Novel

By:

C. C. Blake

Twice Told Tales
2013

San Antonio

This is a work of fiction. Names, characters, places and incidents either are the product of the author's imagination or are used fictitiously, and any resemblance to actual persons, living or dead, business establishments, events, or locales is entirely coincidental. The publisher does not have any control over and does not assume any responsibility for author or third-party websites or their content.

Dedication:

For Glenn and Carlos,
who bought the first one.

For Maurice and Jerry,
who never bought one.

For Lucy and Gary,
who might've read one.

And for Trista,
who's seen them all.

Chapter One

1959

Talc and mothballs did little to mask the smell of death, so Chuck Cave breathed through his mouth.

He sat with his hands in his lap, clasped tight enough to crack his knuckles, but no tension appeared on Chuck's face. His brilliant blue eyes tended to avoid the nearby bed and the man lying in the sweat-stained sheets. Instead, they studied the floor—how clean it was, clear of the cluttering knick-knacks a married man often acquired—while he drew breath after slow breath through his mouth, down his throat, and into his lungs. His instincts would expel these almost the moment he took them in, as though, by keeping the sick man's air too long, Chuck might somehow catch death, too. *Damned foolishness*, he thought before finally meeting the eyes of the man beside him.

Dusk's colors filtered through the drapes, creating angry pink lines on the floor and bed sheets. Dwight Kowalski's face showed few wrinkles, but the light granted him the complexion of aged paper. He resembled some museum mummy, not a friend pushing thirty. His skin looked delicate, as though a strong wind might reduce him to ash sized fragments and whirl, spin, steal him away. Sitting too long at death's door does that to a man.

Though obvious agony constantly lanced through Dwight's frail form, his voice emerged clear as the Mediterranean Sea when he finally spoke. "How is it you never got hooked into the family life?"

Chuck glanced toward the door, as though he might see through it to Dwight's wife. When he had left her, the olive skinned, emerald-eyed woman had been sitting in the hall, thumbing her rosary and whispering the accompanying weighty words. Where was she now? Still there, presumably. Chuck said, "I never had the patience for settling down."

"Does the traveler's life sing so sweetly for you?" Dwight said, and his lips stretched with a wistful smile. "I remember those days. Remember mostly being alone. Sure, there was a kind of freedom, I guess. Then, when we were up there on the Hill, I swore to myself that . . ." His smile faltered. "Plenty of sons died on that fool's errand, huh? And the daughters at home wept . . ." His voice trailed off. There was no need to speak further of the days spent in Korea. Nothing was forgotten. After a moment of troubled silence, his smile returned, "I never really wanted one before the Hill, but after? There was Bea, waiting at home, like some Godsend. And after that . . . Well, Bea loves babies."

"Dolls have a way of making crazy ideas sound reasonable, don't they?"

"That they do." Dwight's chuckle sounded like a hacking cough. "Still, sometimes a woman can make a man see what really matters. Even when he's blind . . ." Chuck moved to protest, but Dwight held a hand to quiet him. "When your guts rebel and start killing you, then you can interrupt, okay? My health problems give me rank in *this* Army." He coughed to clear his throat, but when he spoke next, his voice was even rougher than before. "So, kids aren't for you. But they are for me, I found out. Oh, yes. My boy, Nicholas, and . . . And the one still in the wings. Bea believes this one's to be a girl. Can you imagine? Dwight Kowalski having a little girly?"

"Staggers the imagination," Chuck said.

"I believe her, though. And that little girly's going to be *beautiful*." Another cough made his voice like death personified. "Maybe even more so than her mother." Additional coughing led to momentary choking, and then a wheezing recovery before the spell passed. "I need to know she's taken care of."

Chuck said, "She will be."

"Godfather?" Dwight held his shaking hand out to clasp the deal.

Chuck watched the man's hand tremble like his lips, like his hopes. He stopped squeezing the life from his own hands and found gentleness before taking Dwight's offer. The squeeze proved firm enough. A single shake and it was done, but the men held on for a few more pumps. For old time's sake.

"I'll look after my goddaughter."

Dwight grinned, and the obvious relief washed away a few years, making him the lightly aged version of the man Chuck had met and befriended in Korea. Dwight said, "Thank you, Sarge."

"No thanks needed, pal. You keep fighting this thing. You'll whip it, soon enough."

Dwight's grin transformed into a placating smile. *No*, that expression communicated, *I won't.*

And he did not.

#

1977

When Chuck Cave arrived on the tenement block, he found a crowd of young people—late teens, early twenties—standing along the sidewalks smoking in the afternoon sunshine. As he approached, he nearly gagged at a sickly sweet stink amidst the rough aroma of tobacco, and he knew straight away that most of their cigarettes were joints.

The kids watched him with mixture of guilt and defiance, all too familiar expressions. Most anyone of that age category Chuck ever met held those same mixed responses. As soon as someone leapt over the age of forty, he was a fogey. They considered him even more of a square for the way he carried himself; that disciplined air spoke of a life spent in the military. Particularly after so many young men had been thrown into the meat grinder down in Southeast Asia. An unpopular war—what war was not?—and seemingly unnecessary. The United States was still licking its Vietnam wounds, though they festered from within.

"Hey, pops," one of the kids said. He was the oldest of the lot, maybe twenty-five, and looked like a tanned clown, wearing a sleeveless denim jacket over a broad collared, white shirt open to show off his chest fuzz, pea green slacks tucked into chestnut, knee high boots, and a red bandanna holding up his oily, black jewfro. "What you doing on our block?"

"Walking," Chuck said.

"Yeah, we can see that." The kid elbowed his neighbor and a dozen of them started giggling at once, as though they were not a collection of individuals, but the multiple bodies of a single hive mind. "People like *you* don't usually come a walking through this part of town. Don't you got a job?"

"I'm self-employed," Chuck said. "What's your excuse?"

3

"Self-employed, huh? Well, ain't that funny? *We are, too.* All of us. We're employed to sit on this block and keep eyes out for strangers. Neighborhood watch is what we are. You look like you break into single girls' places and sniff their panties. Maybe jack off on their bedspreads? That what you 'employ' yourself to do?"

Now the hive mind's giggling turned downright mean. Their smiles developed stilettos. Amongst their sniggers, Chuck heard the chatty kid's name: Dexter.

Chuck kept walking. A check of the addresses on the buildings showed his target was the one nearest to the loudmouth and his mass of lost boys and girls.

Dexter, empowered by his hive mind pals, started shouting even louder. "Hey, you a baby butcher, buddy? You *walk* like one. My brother, he was a baby killer, and he winded up getting hisself tits-upped in the rice paddies a year before it was over. Why didn't you stay there, man?" Dexter made *didn't you* sound like *dinchoo.* "Why dinchoo just pull some rice up over your head like a blanket, huh man? You'd have did the world a favor." Additional verbal filth followed this.

His words were difficult to ignore, but Chuck managed. The things coming out of the kids' mouth . . . Where in Hell did this Dexter come up with this stuff? A younger Chuck would have driven a fist into the boy's nose. Crunched the cartilage, filled Dexter's eyes with salty tears, and drowned the boy's leer in lifeblood . . . He—

Those were the actions of a different man. That version could afford to be a hothead, could recover from the retaliation without a hospital stay. He was not that version any more. He was an older model, now. What was it John MacIntire had said to John Wayne? Here it was only two years since he'd seen *Rooster Cogburn,* and Chuck had already forgotten the wording. But he could remember everything Mitch said in *The Friends of Eddie Coyle,* like when he was talking about having four extra knuckles--

You've gone to seed.

Not Mitch's line. That had been what MacIntire's judge had said to the lumbering, one-eyed Wayne. *You've gone to seed.* The judge voicing a generation's worth of exasperation at an old man who refused to sit down already. A man who had spent so long on his own two feet that maybe he didn't know what sitting down even meant, anymore.

Chuck wondered, *Have I gone to seed, too?*

The kids must have picked up on some of his uncertainty because Dexter swatted his buddy saying, "Let's rink it," and then off they went, back along the way Chuck had come.

Chuck scanned the apartment building's mailboxes. Most of them remained unnamed, empty of life, though every window in the building appeared to have someone living behind it. Illegal aliens, maybe. Mexicans hustled across the border to work for peanuts and planted in *el cheapo* apartments. California was firmly rooted in the slave trade, no matter how its politicians preached otherwise.

His thumb paused over the nametag for Room 312. *S. Kowalski*. So far, so lackluster. Chuck knew she could do better than the squatter's heaven slumped before him. He would file this away as one more thing for them to talk about.

The front door opened with the screech of a rape victim. Chuck scowled and stepped into the shadowy foyer. The heat here was worse than outside. Enclosed and without circulation, humidity thickened the air into a choking miasma. Hallways spilled to the right and left, and a door marked "Stairs" stood straight ahead. No sign of an elevator. The nearest doors bore numbers in the one hundreds. The building had five floors. Time for a walk.

#

Three days earlier.

"Chuck?" The bad telephone connection made Bea Kowalski sound quiet as a ghost. A trilling whistle hung ever in the background, as though the voice he heard was not from an honest to God, real human but some kind of a recording.

Chuck had to stuff a finger in his other ear to drown out the Brooklyn racket pouring through his window. "Bea? Well, *hello*. How's—"

"Have you heard from Selma, lately?" Not only the connection but also her tone gave Bea a spectral quality. Her monotone carried all the weariness of Sisyphus, after his first twenty years in Hell. Chuck repressed a shudder.

He had last spoken with Selma a few months before, after she moved to Los Angeles, to an apartment walking distance from the university. She'd talked about making plenty of friends and loving city life and all night coffee shops. Typical stuff.

5

He asked, "Is she alright?"

Only the whistling answered him for ten long seconds. A strange song. Not at all relaxing. Finally, Dwight's widow said, "I don't . . . know."

"What do you mean?"

That whistle, again, this time accompanied by a low roar, as though some poor flutist had been swallowed by a tornado. "I mean," she said, "*I don't know.*"

Chuck's grip on the receiver tightened, making the plastic creak in protest. Inside his mind's eye, he saw Dwight on his deathbed and heard the man's whispered plea for his child's care. Chuck heard himself take the pledge all over again. "Talk to me," Chuck said.

"Couple weeks ago, she went to Mexico with her girlfriends."

Had she gotten lost in that country? "And?"

"And while she was there, she met a man," Bea said. "She called me when she got back to LA."

"This fellow she met . . ."

"I can't recollect his name," Bea said. "It's Allen, I think. But, Chuck . . ."

Again, only the whistle sang for him, and its song was one of dread and loss.

"Bea?"

"I haven't been able to reach her."

"How long since the last time you did?"

"Almost a week. I thought she was . . ." After a moment of quiet, he heard a raspy sound, something like a scratching. Her tongue trying to wet her chapped lips? "I thought she was just spending time with this boy. She's a smart girl, Chuck. She knows how to take care of herself. But she . . ."

The kid certainly did know how to take care of herself, Chuck admitted. Even though she never really got to know him, Selma had intuitively taken after her father.

He asked, "Have you had someone check in on her?"

Bea's response came as a petulant whine. "I don't know anyone down there . . . The numbers I called, her friends' phones . . . They sound like nice girls, but they, they haven't seen her either. They're very nice about it, but I think they're worried."

Hellfire.

"I've been praying that she's all right. I'm scared, Chuck."

"I'll fly out tomorrow," Chuck said. He scanned the stacks of notes around the phone. One of those slips had Selma's building number. Maybe. "Give me her address, again. I'll look in on her."

Relief filled her voice. "Thank you." Then, she recited the address in a despairing monotone.

Though Chuck had been to LA on six occasions, the street name meant little to him. From the brief talk over a long distance connection, Selma had said the neighborhood was very "hip" if "run down."

As it turned out, her words were quite the understatement.

#

1977
Exiting the stairwell to the third floor, Chuck felt as though he had stepped into a sauna. Two windows stood closed at either end of the long hallway. Through them, rusty fire escapes hung like ironwork spiders. Three incandescent lights buzzed down either hall, painting the air itself yellow. Each direction held two-dozen doors arranged so close that only broom closets could stand behind them.

And I thought Brooklyn's buildings were claustrophobic cozy.

Chuck scanned the numbers, turned left and walked to 312.

The carpet, a coarse shag decorated with yellow and black zigzags, squished with every step, and dark, brackish fluid appeared around his shoes, accompanied by the faint scent of sundews. A glance back showed his trail of shoe prints slowly vanishing, swallowed by the carpet once more.

Sweat cascaded down his face and spine, rolling down his arms and legs. *Jesus, what a slum.* The first thing he was going to do was get Selma the hell out of here. Find something a little nicer. If Bea would not or could not front the money for a better place, well, Chuck had some savings he could offer.

"I wouldn't wish this place on my worst enemy," Chuck muttered.

Brass numbers hung on the identical slats of plywood that some contractor might jokingly term "doors." 312 showed plenty of knifepoint graffiti: the initials of lovers wrapped in crude heart shapes, warnings about "The Man" or "Pigs", a random phone number with a San Francisco area code.

When Chuck knocked, the door wobbled in its frame, barely remaining closed. From the other side, a chain lock rattled. A touch revealed the doorknob did not actually move—not locked, it was jammed. Only the slender deadbolt held the door shut. *Wow,* he marveled, *even shit has lower levels to sink to.*

No answer.

"Selma?" he called, "It's Uncle Chuck." He knocked again, harder this time. The door threatened to burst open, so he stopped. *No sense ruining a perfectly lousy door . . .* If he *did,* would the building manager get a proper replacement, or were more of these cheap slabs stacked in the cellar like unwanted corpses?

"*Selma?*"

From further along the corridor, a girl said, "Selma's not there, no more." Chuck glanced over and found a Plain Jane leaning out of a room, three doors away. She was maybe Selma's age, nineteen at most. She wore thick glasses and her dark hair was pulled up into a pair of Afro balls. Dozens of tiny pink hearts decorated her short-sleeved shirt.

"You know where she is?"

She considered him for a moment. "Who'd you say you were?"

"Chuck Cave. I'm Selma's godfather, but she's called me Uncle Chuck since she could call me anything."

The girl smiled, an embarrassed looking thing, and said, "Yeah, she talked about you. You're just like she said you'd be." The girl pointed toward the door at Chuck's back. "She moved to 13 'cause nobody lives there, and the keys are the same."

And shit manages to slide even lower . . .

"But the mailbox—"

"Yeah, we all switch rooms," the girl in room 316 said. "In case someone, you know, tries to mess with us. Selma started the trend. Now, we all do it."

Smart girl. "Thanks," Chuck said. He turned to 313, to knock. The girl from 316 said, "She's not in—" just as his knuckles landed, and the unlocked door swung open.

The orange glow of sunlight through a window shade broke the darkness of the living space beyond. Immediately inside, a pair of narrow doorways opened right and left, forming a hallway of sorts to the main living space.

The left led to a claustrophobic nightmare bathroom. A sink, toilet and bathtub competed for dominance of the room, leaving a body little room to sit or stand. Marks on the walls remained to show where shelves had once been roosted; they had long ago been removed but the holes had not been spackled over to hide the time when this space was enjoying life as a storage closet.

To the right stood the remaining closet. A poorly mounted rod hung askew under the weight of all a girl's colorful clothes. The shelf above sagged from a different load—plenty of weighty, unmarked boxes. Shoes and boots filled the modest floor space.

As Selma's neighbor had said, nobody was home. Chuck asked, "When was the last time you saw her?" but the girl from Room 316 was gone. Her door closed, and the lock clacked shut.

Thanks.

In the living space, he found a light switch glued in place by dried paint globules and yanked it on. A dirt-grimed glass dome in the ceiling flickered to life, casting the room in filthy shadows. The hardwood floor's slats were all scuffed and stained, and the peeling yellow wallpaper offered a sweet stink bouquet of old pot. A bed, bookcase, dresser and vanity packed in a tight configuration crowded the space opposite a narrow stove, pair of cabinets, sink, and flimsy table and chair set.

He spotted familiar gewgaws. Particularly one piece: Mr. Hands. Chuck had found the small wooden figurine of a legless man with oversized hands and a Buddha smile in Acapulco. Selma had fallen in love with it when he gifted it to her. In time it had become her good luck charm. It now sat on the center shelf of her bookcase, surrounded by a chaotic assortment of papers, pencils, notebooks and a dog-eared volume of Plath's poetry.

This was certainly her space.

Chuck swung the door closed behind him and walked to a rather unstable looking wooden chair near the room's lone window. He gave the shade a tug. The lowest plastic edge ripped free before the remainder rolled out of sight above. Outside, a spider web gleamed in the sunlight—beautiful but eerie—completely covering the lowest pane of glass. Its creator sat in the center, surrounded by plentiful bundles of other insects that had come too close for their own good.

Beyond this, the room had an excellent view of a rooftop, a gap indicating the next street over, and another apartment building beyond that. Though the window was anything but sizable, the light it let in filled the entire room. No need for the overhead, Chuck yanked the paint-glommed switch off and returned to the chair.

As he settled down, he realized the damned seat's legs were not even. Slight shifts in weight made the chair rock side-to-side with audible taps. While the motion and sound might be considered soothing, Chuck's current state of mind found it annoying as hell.

He leaned over to look and discovered the fault lay not in the chair but in the floorboards. They were properly aligned but loose.

Did they hide a compartment? A secret place? Somewhere for Selma to keep her valuables, maybe?

Do I have any right to look in there? Probably not.

What if there was valuable information inside? An indication of where she might be? Silent debate raged before he decided to let it remain closed for a while. Keep its secrets. Maybe she was in class, maybe she would return shortly . . . Why not wait?

He glanced at the bedside alarm clock. It was a wind up job, with a pair of bells at the top and a hammer that would rattle between them. Kind of kitschy, actually, in its old fashioned way. Made Chuck smile to see it. So, kids weren't completely removed from yesterday . . .

The thing was silent. The hands had stopped at five twenty three, definitely the wrong time. Was that time in the AM? Even morning classes did not start *that* early . . . She'd wind it before going to bed.

Had she spent the night with her boyfriend? A possibility. Those sorts of clocks, however, did not wind down after only one day. They practiced a policy of steady decrement, the clockworks running for several days before friction took its toll.

So, had she spent a couple of days with her boyfriend?

Again, a possibility, but something in Chuck's gut told him this was not the case. Maybe he was putting Selma on a pedestal of some sort. Maybe he was crediting her with restraint that a teenager would have to be a saint to bear . . . Maybe . . .

The chair wobbled, and the boards beneath it clacked against one another.

Outside, someone pounded on a door. Across the hall? Chuck leaned forward, keeping the chair from rattling against anything.

Silence lasted almost twenty seconds, then that pounding came again. Not quite knocking but definitely across the hall. Selma's room, according to the mailbox.

"She's not there," said the girl from room 316, sounding nervous.

A man's voice said, "You know where she is?"

"Uhm, no—"

Chuck heard clothing rustle, and then the girl squeaked with alarm.

"Don't play games," the man said, and then Chuck heard the telltale click of a gun's hammer being cocked. "And don't try to run, girlie. We'll just break down your door and get what we want anyway."

Chuck stood up. Moved for the door as quietly as possible.

A second voice said, "I dunno, Max. There's plenty of people around—"

"Kids and Mexicanos," the first voice, Max, said, "and they aren't going to do *nada* to save dark meat, here."

Since he had not locked Selma's door, it hung in the jam. Chuck pulled it slowly open, stopping when he could discern three man-shapes in the hall.

"And now that you said my name," Max added, "we have to make sure this little bitch doesn't rat us out."

A door slammed shut, a lock rattled—*good girl*, Chuck thought, *don't let the fear paralyze you*—and the three men laughed.

"Go get her," said Max, and two shapes stomped toward 316.

Chuck pulled open his door. Max turned out to be a fair-haired greaser in his thirties, dressed in long pants and nice shirt, no tie, top button undone. He might have otherwise been a businessman. The shoulder holster and the cocked .45 automatic in his right hand told Chuck his preferred business. Max's lips turned up, at the sound of 313's door opening. "Hey, guys, if that bitch really doesn't know, looks like we've got another volunt—"

Chuck grabbed Max by the head, swung him around and then slammed his face into 313's jam. Max let out a squawk of surprise and dropped his gun. *Good.* Chuck threw him back against 312, and the weary door broke straight down the middle, dumping Max into the empty space beyond.

The two others—also dressed in nice shirts and slacks with automatic pistols in shoulder rigs—now turned from 316's door, which they'd been poised to kick down. One of them had a pencil thin, brown moustache and the other was a towhead. When they saw Chuck's manhandling of their boss, they went for their guns.

Chuck scooped up the fallen .45 automatic and ducked back into Selma's room in time to avoid Max's pals, as they fired a pair of shots from the hip. The girl in 316 started screaming; Chuck hoped she would call the cops.

Of course, the boys in blue would not arrive in time to stop these men, who continued to fire at Chuck's position though they could not see him. *What the hell are they trying to—?*

Of course. The flimsy walls were no sturdier than cheesecloth against the short, stubby .45 caliber rounds. They were blowing holes through the drywall and hoping to catch him by accident.

One of the firing pistols clacked empty, and then the other. Chuck heard the men reloading. He came around low, pistol braced in both hands. The fools were still standing in the open, before 316.

He squeezed off two quick rounds and then returned to cover.

The towhead started shrieking about "My foot. *My motherfucking foot*," before his weight slammed against groaning wood. Not the floor. The gunman had fallen against 316's door. Chuck was putting that girl in danger.

"He's about sixteen inches under where you been aiming," Max said. His voice was nearly comical—with the broken nose, he sounded like he was suffering the world's worst head cold—but he was sitting up on the floor of room 312. Blood poured down his face and he stared daggers at Chuck while playing forward observer for his cronies.

Chuck snapped off a shot at Max. Though the man tried to move, he was on his duff, and therefore pretty slow. The bullet caught him in the left shoulder, and he started squealing like a porcine.

Threaten little girls, will ya?

Any sense of victory Chuck felt vanished, when an automatic pistol started firing again, blowing holes through the wall dangerously close to his position.

The sonsofbitches might be stupid, but they certainly followed orders well. Mr. Pencil Thin Moustache was blazing away about a foot-and-a-half lower than he had been, and luck alone kept Chuck from catching a faceful of slugs.

He scampered deeper into the room, soon realizing it was a deathtrap. If the gunmen played it safe, they could come to the door and open up on him. The room was a barrel and he was the fish. He needed cover. He hopped across the bed. Its springs groaned when he hit them, and then sighed when his weight carried off and onto the other side. Cheap, maybe, but it offered a little more protection than the thin walls.

"Who are you people?" Chuck called.

"Bad company," someone shouted. Must've been Pencil Thin Moustache, since Towhead and Max were still screaming at their pain. "You messing with ba-a-a-ad company."

Give me a break.

Chuck asked, "Want to surrender?" and this got him little more than growls for responses.

Then, the towhead's pistol started firing, punching through still more flimsy building. Not into Selma's room, though. The bastards were up to something else.

When the girl's shrieks got even more desperate, Chuck realized what they were doing. Taking shots through the door of 316. Whether to break in or terrify her, it was impossible to say.

If he did not do something fast, that girl was going to get shot. Alternatively, she would get herself used as a hostage and *then* shot.

Think, damn it. Think.

Chapter Two

Though her hair might have been described as mouse brown, this was the only mousy thing about Selma. Her eyes were set, determined, and her small lips turned down in a frown.

Chuck found her up a tree, sitting on a stout branch, her tiny chin in her palms, fuming as only seven-year old girls could. Closer to the edge of the woods, Bea called her daughter's name. Chuck considered answering, but finally decided to climb the tree in silence, instead.

Young Selma pretended not to notice him, until he arrived at her branch. Then, she turned her shoulders, left-right, left-right, and scooted further out.

"You'll miss your party," Chuck said. "Turning eight doesn't happen all the time, you know."

"I don't care," she said.

"Sure you do," Chuck said. "Your friends are all coming and it'll be tons of fun. Your Mom has spent a lot of time making sure—"

"She always does that. Spends *time*. Makes *sure*." Selma's shoulders rose, to hide the heaving of her sobs. "She doesn't ask me. Not *never*."

"Ask you what?"

"What *I* want. She just . . . She just . . . Does what she wants and expects me to be happy."

Now, the tears started falling. Her small form swayed on the branch, which suddenly appeared much too narrow to hold her, despite the fact that she was a willowy child.

"Well," Chuck asked, "what do you want?"

"I don't want anything. Not anything." She sniffled. "I just want . . ."

Chuck waited, listening to the squirrels and chipmunks and birds, feeling the wind blowing through the leaves, smelling the Pennsylvanian spruce.

"I just want . . ."

After a moment's pause, Chuck asked, "Yeah?"

"*Now you're doing it, too.*" She spun on the branch, an old hat at manipulating her weight so as not to fall. Though tears drew lines down her cheeks and sorrow had a place in her face, rage outweighed it. Not a mere tantrum, this anger was much more . . . *mature.* "I don't need *her.* Or *you.* I don't need *anybody!*"

Chuck fell silent. He was no father, had few words of encouragement. What should he say?

The fury burned away all the sorrow, when she said, "She still cries."

"Your Mom?"

"She cries for him. My Dad. And, I have to hang on to her and tell her 'It's all right.' I . . . I can't cry. I mean, I know it's supposed to be sad and everything, but I never knew him. For me, he's never been any different than he is, now. But Mommy cries for him. Sometimes. A lot. And I have to tell her 'I love you, Mommy. I'm sorry and it's awful but *I* love you, and I'm right here.'" She shook her head, and the leaves on the branch rustled. "And then she pretends I need her to do stuff for me . . . I don't *need* anything or anybody!"

"No, you probably don't," Chuck said. "You're pretty strong. Amazingly strong, sometimes."

Uncertainty shoved some of the anger aside. "Really?"

"Really."

Fury softened, then. "So, will you make her believe me?"

Chuck sighed, and the act shifted his weight so that he almost fell. Selma gasped, but he caught another branch and stabilized himself.

She said, "Don't climb trees much, huh?"

"Not anymore," he said. "When I was growing up outside Pontiac, Michigan, yeah. Then I got *real* old."

"You're not *that* old."

"From your lips to God's ears."

She started smiling when he said that. It was a common response from her.

He asked, "Why's that funny?"

She shrugged. In a few years, when he asked her that same question, she would surprise him; however, it would still be a while before she would be able to find the words to compose a meaningful answer.

Her smile demanded an echo from him, and they shared a pleasant moment of quiet as July sunlight filtered through the green leaves, anointing her face with gold. Her's was an earnest expression, filled with hope and a longing to be understood. She needed a real father, not a once-in-a-while visitor, a godfather from New Yak. In that instant, Chuck recalled his pal's deathbed words about being blind to what you really want, about women pushing for good decisions, and about having a kid of his own. But it was already too late. *I'm much too old to be starting out. And too alone.*

"You're a pretty great kid, you know that Selma?"

"Huh?"

"Takes a lot to be able to see your Mom crying and not be afraid. To say nice things to her and love her."

Selma tried to turn away, to hide her embarrassment. "Nah. I don't know. Whatever. I guess."

Chuck tilted his head back to hide his own smile.

"So, if I'm so strong, can you tell her I don't need her to be so . . . You know . . . *Coddled* all the time?"

"I'm afraid not, kiddo," Chuck said. "I know you're tough. You know your tough. But can you pretend? Your mom . . . She needs to be needed, if that makes any sense."

Selma considered this, as another wind blew, carrying the smell of blooming hyacinths and wild flowers.

"I— I guess."

"She'll appreciate it," said Chuck. "Maybe I can convince her to lay off a little."

"Thanks, Uncle Chuck."

"Now, how's about helping me out of this tree?"

#

1977

Chuck had spent three rounds. That would leave four in the magazine, providing Max was playing with a full mag. No time to check, there was only time to hope. Paint chips and drywall dust spat out of the wall where he had crouched only seconds before; Mr. Pencil Thin Moustache continued drilling .45 caliber holes through the walls, into Selma's closet.

Not only the girl in 316 was shouting. Now, people on the floors below, around and above were getting excited. Panicking.

And there was only seconds to save that girl.

Max was screaming for them to kill someone, anyone, just kill, and Chuck wished his bullet had caught that sucker in the head.

Then, Mr. Pencil Thin Moustache's pistol ran dry. A plan came to mind, and he ran with it. Chuck was up, over the bed, and his hard soles pounded against the floorboards as he raced for the door.

Outside, he heard Pencil Thin Moustache's curses and fumbled reloading. Chuck made it to the door and jumped across the hall, just as the dark haired man pulled the slide to jack a fresh clip's first round into the chamber.

The .45 coughed flame. A bullet passed through the air beneath Chuck in the instant before he cleared the hallway and landed in Room 312. Max heard him crash onto the floorboards, and his eyes were filled with equal parts fury and agony, as he clenched his shoulder and called for his boys to, "Come get 'im! He's in here with me!"

Chuck scootched closer to the downed man and dragged him to his feet. When Mr. Pencil Thin Moustache arrived, Chuck held Max like a human shield, pistol held at Max's temple.

"Drop the gun," Chuck said, "or Max here will need a whole lot of shit to fill the hole I'm gonna make."

Mr. Pencil Thin Moustache hesitated, his wide eyes moving from Chuck to Max and back again, gun hand trembling. He muttered something that might have been, "It wasn't supposed to be like this."

"It never is," Chuck said. "*Hey, towhead*," he called. "*Stop the shooting or Maxy-boy gets his head blown off.*"

The towhead must've heard because the firing stopped, and he asked, "Max?"

"Kill 'im," Max snarled, words flecked with foamy saliva. "I said—" Snarls turned into screams when Chuck squeezed the wounded man's shoulder.

Chuck said, "Sounds pretty bad, there, Max. You're gonna need a whole lot of hospital time."

"I'm gonna kill you, mother—" Words disintegrated again, becoming unintelligible screams as Chuck applied more pressure.

"I've got no respect for men trying to kill little girls," Chuck said, "Even less for a joker who needs to mastermind two more tough bastards with guns to do it." He crushed Max's shoulder again, and the man squirmed in torment.

"S-stop it," Mr. Pencil Thin Moustache said. "Don't do that—"

"I make the rules here," Chuck said. "So tell me what you people are doing. Tell me what you want with Selma."

"Don't tell him *nothing*," Max said, "Or you'll—" More pressure, more screams.

"Who you gonna listen to?" Chuck said.

Mr. Pencil Thin Moustache's face filled with fresh sweat, and it was not born solely from the heavy atmosphere. "I—":

"You were looking for Selma?"

"Yeah. We—"

"God damn it, Francis, shut your—" Fury filled this batch of Max's screams.

"Francis," Chuck said, "you were saying?"

Francis said, "Here to get her."

"And you were going to tell me why?"

"She's holding out on something."

"Francis, damn it—"

"What's she holding, Francis?"

"A package."

"From who?"

Max said, "If you tell, I'll—"

"*From who?*"

Francis said, "From Allen—"

"Shut your mouth," Max said.

"Allen? Her boyfriend, Allen?"

If someone had spontaneously gut punched Francis, he would not have looked so surprised. "Boyfriend?"

"Allen who?"

"For Christ's sake, Francis, I'll fucking kill you myself if you—"

"Tell me, Francis. Save your bossy buddy here from his own stupidity."

Francis shook his head.

"You want me to kill him, Francis?" Chuck asked. "If I do that, I'm gonna kill you next."

"Lang," Francis said. "Allen Lang."

"God damn you, Francis," said Max.

To Chuck, Francis said: "Let him go, okay?" Then, he licked his lips and said, "Max, I—"

Fully automatic weapon's fire eradicated Francis' words, and turned him into a spinning dervish of death.

As one, Chuck and Max said, "*Shit.*"

Chuck asked, "Who the hell is that?" as Max said, "The Devil's guys! We're dead, men. Dead!"

More bursts echoed through the hallways, and the towhead's screams ceased.

"They're gonna kill us," Max said, terror foisting off his pain. "We have to get out of here, man. Outsville or we are *out*."

Chuck heard the sounds of solid soles sauntering toward them. *Cold as cucumbers*, Chuck thought, *whoever these gunmen are, they're certainly cold and callous enough to be professionals.*

"You've got an extra clip?" Chuck asked.

"Three," Max said.

"Give me one."

Max reached with his right arm and curled in pain—the wound, of course—though he managed to stay relatively quiet. "Can't," Max said.

Hellfire.

The footsteps slowed, were they nearing the smashed door? He considered the sounds and aimed the pistol for the wall beside the door jam. If it worked for the no nothing Mr. Pencil Thin Moustache and the Towhead, it'd probably work for him, too.

The footstep paused, and Chuck took the shot. Paper and plaster dust burst from the wall, as the slug punched through the materials. From the other side, Chuck heard a startled grunt and some jabbered words of warning. Then, a man appeared in the doorway, bleeding from his shoulder, but still holding a Schmeisser submachinegun. He was a stern-faced fellow, with a look not of surprise but resignation on his face. This guy was dead and knew it, but still he tried to level his weapon at Chuck.

Chuck popped a round in the man's forehead, an instant before the gunman's finger jerked the trigger; lead death spat out the muzzle, tearing a line of holes through the ceiling. *Hope to Hell everyone cleared out from up there*, Chuck thought. When the man's leather soles showed, Chuck shoved Max to the side. There was no furniture in this room, no cover but the closet and the bathroom. It was an even easier kill zone than Selma's actual room.

"Hey, hero man," Max said and slid a pair of clips across the floor. He'd slipped out of the shoulder rig enough that he could unclip the spare mags with his unwounded hand. Unfortunately, he was entangled by his own shoulder holster. It was all he could do to slide the clips over, and then he was stuck on his belly, his head in clear line of sight of the door.

Gunman number two took advantage of this, and a three round burst caught Max across the ear, blowing messy holes through the man's skull and sending him straight to his reward.

"Hellfire," Chuck whispered, but snatched up the clips. No time to reload. Only two rounds left, providing Max was playing with a full clip. If there was only one guy, then—

The submachine gun spat more death, and fresh holes ripped through the walls. So, the SOB had learned from his buddy's mistake. Of course, the gunman had seen Max's valiant effort to share ammo, so the holes appeared about waist level for a standing Chuck. Crouched as he was, the rounds probably would have blown his own head into the same Chinese Hell of Many Holes as Max, but luckily he was leaning for the clips, hunkered too low to catch lead.

Chuck counted the cartridges remaining in his clip while the enemy's brass thup-thup-thupped against the moist, cheap carpet in the hallway outside. Shit, the hallway floor was wet, wasn't it? Not the rooms, though. They were bone dry.

Blake

The enemy's weapon clacked empty, and the man's shoes made squishy sounds across the floor, as he backed up, presumably behind cover. Chuck used the opportunity to roll across the room to Max's side. He slid alongside the dead man, smelling the splattered head contents. His stomach heaved in protest. What the hell had he gotten in the middle of?

From the hallway, a fresh clip clacked home and the enemy jacked the first cartridge into the chamber, and then began to chew still more holes into the wall where Chuck had been hiding. By now, that wall and the closet between it and the hallway, looked like a wooden approximation of Swiss cheese. Was there still anywhere a human being could hide in such a holey mess?

Regardless, the fellow continued training his fire, now at about knee level to a standing man. If Chuck had not left that position, he would certainly be dead by now.

The enemy's weapon once more clacked empty, and the carpet squished as the fellow moved back—presumably behind cover—to reload.

Chuck used the opportunity as well. Better a full mag than one round.

Weapons clacked, as both men chambered fresh rounds. The guy did not immediately open fire again, though. "You're still alive, huh?" the fellow said. He had a strange quality to his voice, a lightness to the words, like Chuck had heard in some of the more Northern Midwestern states. The Scandinavian sounds of the Dakotas, Minnesota, Wisconsin, "Da Yooper Penninsula" of Michigan.

"There's two dead out here," the gunman said, "and I splattered that third one's brains pretty good, don't you know." *Prit-tee gewd, donchaknow*? "There ain't supposed to be four. What's say, you explain yourself, huh buddy?"

Did this guy really think that'd work?

Chuck hazarded a glance around the corner. The door's jam was blow to hell, as was most of the closet, and quite a bit of the hallway. Of particular interest to Chuck, though was the light switch. It hung in a cluster of drywall, like the head of a flower; the stalk was a bunch of poorly maintained, fraying wires, which descended into the floorboards, probably to the next apartment. One good shot might just sever those electricity lines . . . Once they were off the switch, though, they'd be live wires. 110 volts of danger.

The gunman said, "There ain't a whole hell of a lot of wall left for you to hide behind. Sooner as later I'll pop your lights. Might as well leave your legacy." He chuckled. "Or share your benediction?"

Chuck aimed Max's pistol, felt the sweat beading on his brow. Missing was not an option, but if he did not do this just right, he was as good as dead. The gunman would know he'd moved, and would start popping holes through this fresh surface. Sure, the bathtub on the other side of the wall might slow down the whittling process some, but not terribly much.

Hard to suck in the hot, humid air, so Chuck stopped breathing. Closed his eyes, calmed himself, opened them again. Why the hell did he bother reloading?

One shot would be more than enough.

No time to get cocky. He aimed, did the mental geometry and then squeezed. Hammer slammed down on the primer cap, which ignited the gunpowder. Gasses built until they forced the cartridge out of the brass, and the cartridge spat out at high velocity. It hit the electricity lines, which ripped apart, falling back into the wall, bouncing off a stud, and then out again.

Right onto the room's dry wooden floor.

Hellfire. If he threw the gun . . . No, there was no guarantee the small handgun would do anything to move those wires. He needed something bigger. No furniture, this room was pretty barren. Except for . . .

The guy laughed, now. "You missed me, jerk. And now I know right where you are . . ."

Chuck hefted Max's corpse by belt and neck. He twisted at the waist so that Max's ass touched the wall. Like a coiled spring, he untwisted, whipping Max's body before him, feeling the burn in his arms.

Physicists say centrifugal force is an illusion. They say that the only measurable force is not aimed outward, but toward the center of a rotating object. Illusion or not, when Chuck let go, the body flew from him, crashed onto the wooden floor five feet away, bounced and rolled into the hallway.

Dragging the cut electrical line as it went.

Chuck discovered a whole new kind of stink: the carpet was burning, as was whatever aqueous sludge has soaked it, as was the gunman standing on the soaked carpet. Then, somewhere in the basement, the fuse blew, and all the lights went out. A heavy weight fell to the floor with a *slush* sound, and for a moment, the world was quiet.

Chuck could sit and breathe, but he could not bring himself to stop looking at the puddle of blood on the floor.

What in Hell was going on? What had Selma gotten mixed up in? It was enough to make a man's head spin. Or get it blown clean off.

Blake

A door squawked open—room 316—and the girl shouted, "Is it over?"

Chuck called back, "Stay inside," waited for her door to clack shut, the lock to engage, and then he moved to find out.

Max lay on the floor of the hallway, staring at the ceiling with his dead man's eyes. The holes through his head were leaking all sorts of viscous fluids. Chuck tried not to stare, to stare too long would bring up his lunch. Past him, partially landed in Selma's real room was the first gunman, bloody shoulder and head wound. It was like the man had three eyes, two placed in the natural positions and the last slightly up and to the left of center.

Through the holes in the wall, he could not make out the second gunman. The pistol was heavy in Chuck's slick hand, but still he held it steady as he came around the door, partially entering the hallway.

Even more sludge stained the hallway carpet. The second gunman was quite dead, and he looked a bit like Chuck had expected. A fair haired fellow, broad shouldered, Nordic featured. His nose was crooked from one too many improperly tended breaks, and his lips were stretched in a lunatic's grin. In death, he'd soiled himself. The electricity jolt had clenched every muscle in his body. When the fuse blew, all those muscles relaxed. Any fluids they were holding back evacuated. Urine and feces and snot and . . . Still, that smile gave Chuck a shiver. *I'll see you soon*, that smile said, *down here in the warm place where men like us all wind up.*

Men like us . . .

"I'm nothing like you," Chuck whispered. Then, he called to 316, "It's all over."

That door cracked open, once more, and the girl inside looked out. Her face was the color of ash, and her cheeks were stained with tear tracks. Her whole body was wracked with shakes and shivers.

"Are you all right?" It was a stupid question, Chuck knew. Of course she was anything but all right . . . Still, he did not know what else to ask.

"I— I'm . . . not shot."

"I'm glad," Chuck said. "Neither am I."

"These men. You . . . You killed . . ." She looked down at the mess of the towhead, and could not restrain herself. "Oh. Oh *God*." Vomit spilled over her lips and down onto the submachine gun blasted pile of meat. She started weeping more heavily, now.

Chuck stood up, transferred the pistol to his left hand and hid it alongside his leg. "Hey, you. Girlie. Look at me." When she did, she looked shell shocked. "I can't call you Girlie," Chuck said, "What's your name?"

"Marlie," she said. "Marlie Todd."

"Well, Marlie Todd, I need you to keep looking at me, okay? And I need you to come here." He held his hand toward her. "Don't look at them, just stand up. Walk over here. Can you do that?"

She shook her head.

"Why not, Marlie?"

"I— I can't *move*."

Chuck said, "Sure you can. Let's take it a bit at a time, okay?" He hunkered, and her eyes moved to the corpses at his feet. "*Marlie*. Look at me, okay? At my eyes. See them?"

"You. You got hard eyes, Mister."

"I suppose I do. But we're going to stand up, okay? I'll move a little then you, we'll do it together. Don't leave me hanging half way, alright?"

"I— I—" She looked ready to cry.

"You can do it, Marlie. You can do it." He started to rise from the hunker. "Just slow and easy and—Dammit, Marlie, *don't stop looking at my eyes*. That's better. Now just . . . Don't leave me hanging. Good. A little more, and . . . You're up!" He smiled, but she did not. "Now come on over. Come on."

She looked doubtful, started to glance back down.

"No, Marlie, don't—"

"I— Have to," she said, "or I'll trip and land on him. My God, they're all dead. They were going to kill me, and now they're all dead." She stepped over the body, and though her knees threatened to fall out from under her, they held her up.

Kids didn't need anyone anymore, did they?

Chuck's hand dropped. "I'm sorry if I've been treating you like a child."

"But that's all I am to you, right?" Marlie said, voice empty of emotion. "A little girl?"

Chuck said nothing. Marlie walked up alongside him, grabbed his hand and squeezed it with ten times more strength than Chuck thought she might have. "Maybe," she said, "just for right now, it's okay to be . . . a child." He squeezed her hand back, and a small amount of relief softened the horror on her face.

Chuck got her to the stairwell door, told her to wait, opened it, and then checked it for danger. No additional gunmen waited, only some folks from the next floor up who were trying to descend slowly and quietly. When they saw Chuck's gun, they waved their palms in surrender, speaking rapid fire Spanish at him. "*No molestes*," he said and waved them on.

Blake

To Marlie Todd, he said, "It's all clear. You want me to come with you all the way down?"

She stared into his eyes, and he saw a hardness in the blues that wasn't there before. "You're not going to profane them, are you?"

"I need some answers. They were here after Selma."

"They won't have any answers."

"I won't touch them. I just have to get something from Selma's room."

"Mr. Hands?"

He thought again about that good luck charm, the wooden figurine who had traveled all the way from Acapulco?

"Yeah," he said. "Mr. Hands."

"Wouldn't want nobody to steal it."

"Nope."

A ghost of a smile graced her lips, and she nodded. "I'll be all right."

He watched her go, let the door clack shut behind her, and then walked back past the bodies and into Selma's room, praying that whatever she'd hidden in her secret place would be somehow helpful . . .

Chapter Three

1972

Selma was much happier than her mother to see New York City. At age thirteen and coming from a small town like Drucker's Meadow, Pennsylvania, the "beeg city" must have seemed a mighty, peculiar, scary, spectacular place, indeed.

Even for Bea, the city made quite the impression, although without a doubt that impression was of the negative variety. Chuck had taken a day off to show them some of the bigger sights, the Statue and the Empire and Central Park. Whenever a black man looked their way, or a Chinese or a Japanese or anyone that wasn't obviously white (and for some reason, this also included at least one or two Italians), Bea's hand would tighten on her daughter's shoulder, ready to yank her out of harm's way.

Truth be told, Selma had been enraptured by just about everything, but the one thing that completely sparked her imagination had been the subway. When Chuck asked her, "Why?" she answered,

"I've never seen anything like this before." She blushed a little, when she added, "The Liberty Lady is nice and all, but a statue is just a statue. And the Empire State Building is really tall, but it's just a building. We've got both of those—statues and buildings—in Drucker." Indeed, Drucker's Meadows did have statues and buildings, Chuck admitted, though neither were quite as impressive.

"But a train that runs underground and takes you all over?" Her jaw practically dropped in sheer amazement. "That's pretty cool. Heck, Drucker doesn't even have *buses*."

"Surely you must've seen the subway on television."

"Uh-huh. I mean, *yeah*. Of course. But seeing isn't *riding*?" She giggled. "And all them guys wearing no shirts under their sheepskin coats? Pretty cool."

Bea whispered something, and Chuck asked her, "What?"

"I could never stand the city. So large, so many places for a body to get lost . . ." She shook her head. "Lord save us from the city."

"You maybe," Selma said, "but not me. I like this place. Maybe I'll move here when I get older."

Chuck cracked a grin, and Bea looked pretty thoroughly horrorstruck. Selma turned on her innocent face, widening her blue eyes to enormous proportions, making her mouth as small as possible, and cocking her head to one side. "Did I say something wrong, Mom?"

Now it was Bea's turn to blush, and no matter how much she obviously longed to, she did not break contact with her daughter's eyes. "I— I had no idea that you wanted . . . Wanted to come to a place like this."

"Huh," Selma said.

"I'm surprised," Chuck said, "but maybe not as much as your Mom. The city has a way of charming a mind."

"You must love it here," Selma said. "So much to do and see."

"Actually," Chuck said, rubbing his jawline, "I don't get to see much of it."

"Work?"

Chuck nodded. "The company doesn't sit still. They send me all across the country. Last week, this time, I was in San Francisco. Next week, it's up to central Massachusetts. Week after that? Maybe I'll stick around here, but then it's off to Baton Rouge or Detroit, El Paso or Kansas City . . . Nah, when I get back here, it's usually enough time for me to rest my head from whatever jet lag, travel weariness I've sucked up on the latest jag, and getting ready to go somewhere else."

"You mean you don't see the stuff we saw today?"

"Nah," Chuck said, shaking his head slowly, thoughtfully, "this stuff is mostly for tourists. Living and working in this city's not quite the same as visiting it."

"That's so sad," Selma said. "I don't ever want to be so busy with a job that I can't see stuff."

"It happens to everyone," Bea said.

"Not to me, Mom."

"We'll see," Chuck said.

They walked on, and Chuck bought them hotdogs from a street corner vendor. Selma kept requesting more condiments, until the vendor said, "Are you trying to make me go bust on ketchup?"

When Selma bit into the slathered dog, Chuck half expected her to squint or blanch or pucker, the typical result of too much of a good thing. Instead, she was in overindulgent heaven and smiling fit to beat the band.

"I had no idea," Bea said, "that my own daughter could eat such quantities of garbage."

Chuck glanced back, to make sure the vendor was out of earshot, and Selma said, "I guess there's a lot you don't know about me, Mom."

Bea, ever the exasperated mother, said, "I guess so."

#

1977

Chuck stepped over the corpses and into Selma's room. His shoes left red trails across the hardwood. Despite the loose boards it rested upon, the chair did not appear crooked, someone had taken competent care to disguise them.

He knocked the chair aside and knelt over the boards. His fingernails found the seams, easily enough, but the actual prying up required more effort than he initially suspected.

The weight was all wrong. They slid away from the pressure he applied, and he soon found yet another problem. Though the boards appeared shaped in two inch wide slats, like the rest of the floor, each of these was merely the surface cover for an unknown number of interconnected braces underneath. These made the thing a reverse puzzle, one decidedly more difficult to pull apart than put together. He took nearly three minutes to free one three-inch long, two-inch wide board. Instead of trying for the next proper board, he used the chair leg to hammer the rest apart. Fifty second later, he had a mostly cleared out hole onto the secret place.

What expectations he had did not approach what actually lay within. His brows furrowed, and his lips pressed into a tight line. *What do we have here?*

Immediately visible was a notebook, the red cover of which featured the white smears that came about when someone rubbed a pencil eraser in steady strokes. These smears formed letters, a title, perhaps, spelling out "The Devil's Manifesto." Chuck flipped through this, found page after page decorated with tight, blue, ball point pen script. The loops on letters like 'l', 'y' or 'g' were so tight as to be nonexistent, a meticulous, masculine scrawl, certainly not Selma's carefree hand. Interspersed among this, someone had pasted six newspaper clippings. All of these were on violent subjects. A building fire from last year that claimed three lives, an as yet unsolved murder case almost four years old, an automobile accident where some commuter car had struck a big rig hauling gasoline and ended as a fireball, the gang beating and rape of a wheelchair bound woman and her nurse, a piece on a federal bust of a drug shipment coming into the country from Mexico, and the double suicide of a moderately important counterculture figure and his male lover.

Beneath the notebook was a plastic baggie containing a single brass key. A housekey, maybe? This found its way into Chuck's pocket.

Beneath these lay a square parcel wrapped in brown paper, approximately one foot to a side, covered with HR Puffenstuff stickers, and bound in thick twine.

When Chuck pulled this out, it proved to be almost five inches thick and surprisingly light. First glance made the package seem like something sturdy and weighty, like some wrapped cinderblock. In truth it weighed only a few pounds. Chuck's pocketknife made short work of the twine. The paper showed no seams on the top, so he flipped it over and laid it on the bed. A seam ran down this side, pinned shut by the sticker of some green-faced humanoid cartoon character with a fat cigarette hanging from between his lips.

Chuck slid his pocketknife along the seam, breaking the sticker in half, and the paper practically unwrapped itself. Inside, Chuck found half a dozen individual packages, some kind of dark, organic material wrapped in Saran Wrap. A quick snip from a pair of nearby scissors let the contents out. Leaves and seeds, a tell-tale smell.

Marijuana?

He fell onto his duff, as though sucker punched. *Jesus, kiddo*, he thought again, *what the hell did you get involved in*?

Outside, he could hear approaching sirens. Should he just let them find this here? Would they think Selma was somehow involved? Then again, the contraband had Chuck's fingerprints all over it, and his shoeprints tracked blood from the hall to the hole.

Hellfire. He was already in this too far. This much dope was a felony. Would the cops believe anything he had to say?

On the flip side of that coin, did he really want to hand this matter over to the cops? Wash his hands of the responsibility of finding out exactly what was going on here?

What was he considering, otherwise?

As the ceaseless, screaming sirens closed in, he closed his eyes and squeezed the bridge of his nose. The applied pressure was certainly clarifying. He recalled Dwight on his death bed, recalled the words they had exchanged. It might not have been an out and out *promise*, but he had still made a pledge.

He muttered a curse. Scooped up the drugs and the notebook. These he dumped into a canvas laundry sack along with the pistol and several handfuls of Selma's dirty clothes to pad the contraband out. After this, he hustled to the hall, pausing to pick up a couple more clips for the pistol, and then he was down the stairs and out, trying like mad to vacate the scene before the cops arrived.

Marlie saw him on the way out the front door, as the black and whites turned onto the street.

He met her eyes, thought about stopping. She looked away from him, toward the cops, giving him permission to go.

He thanked her under his breath, turned up the street and started walking.

#

1974

No one was more surprised than Chuck to find a rather pretty, bleach blonde girl on the doorstep of his apartment building at nearly midnight, looking bleary eyed and terrified. When she said, "Hi, Uncle Chuck," he realized she was Selma.

Jesus, how she had grown. She was fifteen but already looked several years older than that. Maybe it was the clothes, which showed too much, or the makeup, which was sparse but carefully applied to emphasize her natural attractiveness.

The first thing out of his mouth was "What the Hell are you doing here?"

She tried to diffuse the situation with a smile. It trembled too much though, suggesting she had played witness to the neighborhood's less than savory elements. "Can I come in?"

He fumbled after his key and brought her up to his third floor apartment, an orderly-looking three room place with the qualities of a museum: often visited but never quite lived in. As soon as he closed and locked the door, Selma stopped shaking quite so much.

"Does your mom know you're in Brooklyn?"

"Nope." Nervous laughter accompanied this answer. "She doesn't know *anything*."

"And what are you doing here?"

She bit her lip, an old habit, but did not answer.

"Well?" he prompted.

She released her lip and the words came out of her mouth in a thunderous blurt: "IwanttolivewithyouUncleChuck."

Chuck sank into a comfortable chair, undoubtedly staring with the same state of shock he might have, had she spontaneously grown a second head. "You . . . What?"

She simply repeated what she had already said, slower this time. "I want to live with you, Uncle Chuck."

"I guess I did hear you right," he brushed his fingertips across his forehead. "But . . . Why?"

"Drucker's Meadow is nice and all, but . . . Well, you know. It's nowhere's 'ville. And Mom's always . . ." She shrugged as though this should all be self-evident, before concluding with another rendition of that classic: "You know."

"No, sweetie, I don't. Tell me."

"She's . . . Remember when I turned eight, and you told me to pretend that I needed her? Well, I've been pretending, and I know you talked to her . . . Whenever we're around you or Bill, she's okay, but otherwise, she's a real mess. A real mess."

"Who's Bill?"

"Mom's new, uhm, boyfriend."

"Ah. Serious?"

"No, I think he only wants her for sex."

Chuck blinked a few times. He had already been surprised by how different Selma looked, now it was the way she talked. She'd always been mature for her age, but Jesus, when had Selma grown up?

"When you or Bill are around, she's star-eyed. When we're alone, Mom's still crying and . . . She's a big hassle."

"So you want to move in with me?"

Selma gave a single but assertive nod. "You bet. I can clean up and . . . Well, you don't really need much of that, huh?"

"Remember when you came here, a few years ago? I told you the company sends me all over the country. They still do."

"Well, we can work around that," she said.

"Oh, can we?"

"You're a pretty resourceful guy."

Chuck laughed, really more of an exhale. "Your lips to God's ear."

She giggled at this.

"Why is that funny?" he asked.

She shrugged, but her eyes turned up as she considered the question. After a moment, she said, "Because Mom never says stuff like that. With her, God isn't someone you talk to, except to ask forgiveness from. To ask forgiveness and expect punishment."

"I see," Chuck dragged his hand across the seven o'clock shadow over his jaw. "Kiddo, I hate to break it to you—"

"You're going to tell me I can't stay, right?" There was no small amount of pain in her voice. "Because you're a busy guy, and you worry that you'll be gone too much?

"You always were a smart cookie."

"Well, can you at least let me spend the night, Uncle Chuck? Tell me there's no room for me in your life, tomorrow?"

He thought about this. "I can't very well kick you out at a gahdawful hour like this."

"Thanks," she said.

"Kiddo," he said, "if it's really so rough at home, maybe I can—"

"I'm kind of tired, Uncle Chuck. Should I sleep over there?" She pointed to the couch.

"Sure," he said.

In the morning, they did not speak of her staying, again.

#

1977

Back at his hotel room, Chuck looked at the collection of oddities and wondered, *What do I have here? Where do I go from here?*

He had a hell of a lot of drugs. He had a firearm that could be traced to several murders. He had a notebook filled with ramblings—not many of which made any coherent sense. He had two names: Allen Lang and "The Devil." The notebook also had that second name "The Devil" featured prominently on its cover.

Names. Allen Lang and the Devil. Lang and the Devil.

Well, despite the outrageous name, this "Devil" certainly hired a better class of killer. Not the bumblers that apparently worked for this Lang fellow. *Devil.* A man did not choose a name of that caliber without seeking to strike fear in the hearts of others.

Did the drugs belong to him? How did Selma get her hands on them? How did Selma figure into this whole bloody affair. Lang's men came to call on her old apartment, the Devil's men showed up only minutes later. All of them were armed for one thing: murder.

The cause? Selma was holding. Selma had the drugs. Everything came back to those bricks of dope. Little Selma had certainly grown up and gotten neck deep in some serious trouble.

He flipped through the notebook again, read passages and eyed those clippings a little more closely.

Last year's building fire, he discovered, was of a supposed drug house. Not just flopspace, the building and its owners were suspected to be involved in the receipt of smuggled narcotics (most marijuana) as well as cleaning, packaging, storing, and selling. Dope central, the clipping called it. It had been under federal observation for a week and then mysteriously destroyed by fire, and the three suspected primary operators did not escape the flames with their lives. Arson. Murder. Committed by rival dope pushers, maybe?

The scrawl written beneath this piece declared it "The first of The Rose Devil's sinful sacraments: Invocation."

The Rose Devil? Sinful sacraments? Chuck had the strongest suspicions that neither the deed nor the being this writer blamed these events on was, in fact, some supernatural entity . . .

The murder case clipping detailed a butchered LA businessman, a financier of adult films and the owner of a local nightspot, The D*O*G House, who had been found in three different garbage bags across town. A job, the reporter opined, worthy of the great Mickey Cohen some twenty years earlier. However, at the time of the article, a review piece written some two weeks after the crime, a lack of leads and clues forced police to leave this one in the unsolved files. The journalist, byline: Chet Williams, further opined that too many crimes (and thinly veiled allegations of corruption) could close out even the most brutal crimes as insoluble.

The notebook's author declared this murder to be "The second of The Rose Devil's sinful sacraments: Evocation."

Did that make this nightclub owner and film financier linked to drugs, too?

The automobile/gas semi collision seemed routine enough. At eleven thirty pm, a sedan jumped lanes into oncoming traffic and the side of a gasoline truck. The car's driver and two passengers died in the flames, and the truck driver went to the hospital with serious burns and broken limbs. Police suspected the auto's driver had been drinking.

The unidentified author of The Devil's Manifesto believed it to be of a much more sinister origin. "The third of the Rose Devil's sinful sacraments: Manifestation of the Will. Robbie asked too much and looked too closely. Pentathol in the Quaaludes and car keys did the work that a bullet might have been questioned for."

So, dead driver "Robbie" was asking after this Rose Devil or maybe just the drug, and the Devil doesn't merely shoot him or send one of his deadly effective gunmen? He decides to give this Robbie fellow some kind of polluted drugs and then hope he drives into a semi? It seemed not only unlikely and impractical but damned stupid.

Unless, a cold part of Chuck's mind—the reptilian section, the killer inside—said, *he had the inside skinny to verify the kill.* What if the drugs knocked out this Robbie, and then one of the Devil's men made it look like an accident?

The gang rape and beating of the wheelchair bound woman and her nurse. A horrible crime, both were left alive, but the wheelchair woman was left comatose and the nurse nearly drowned on a rag soaked some kind of noxious, but unnamed fluid.

"The fourth of the Rose Devil's sinful sacraments: Cutting the Ties," the Devil's Manifesto said, "The Rose Devil trades in carnality, and she who sired the Antagonist would remain forever stripped of all but the most basic form of life."

The Antagonist? Did that mean the Rose Devil? Or Lang? Would the Rose Devil have his own mother so assaulted? Or was the victim Lang's mother? What kind of sociopath would orchestrate such awfulness? If it *was* Lang's mother, how did he retaliate for this assault? And what happened to the Nurse? The victims for these crimes were always overlooked by both this Devil and the author of the book. And were they two individuals? Could author of both the Manifesto *and* crimes be one and the same?

The fifth article detailed the federal interception of a small aircraft flying into the United States from South America (last stop had been somewhere in Mexico). In its hold, a baker's dozen crates of dope, street value estimated to be two hundred thousand dollars.

"The fifth of the Rose Devil's sinful sacraments: Enslavement of the Ambitious. The Devil's aids," the Manifesto auteur wrote, "know better than to question His orders. None in this world's seats of power are free of sin, and who but the Rose Devil has such thorough files on all the sinning of the world? He Knows Much, if not All . . ."

Chuck's instinctive response to this was "Horseshit." However, upon further consideration, he had to admit that plenty of corruption found its way into positions of power. Life had seemed so much more simple when he was a boy. He knew who was wrong and who to blame, but returning from Korea to these United States offered him more shades of uncertainty, a gray coloration to politics and economics and right and wrong. So much, he sometimes thought he might lose his mind . . .

Still, that last comment about The Rose Devil being some kind of omniscient blackmailer struck him as more than a little bit of grand standing.

On that last article, detailing the double suicide of a moderately important counterculture figure and his male lover, the police declared it to be a self-evident case. Journalist Chet Williams offered more inferences of murder and corruption, while the Devil's Manifesto author offered his most cryptic notation yet:

"The sixth of the Rose Devil's sinful sacraments: Transcendence of Flesh. As my life ends, so it shall endure. Forever and ever. Nema."

Chuck closed the book, stewing over the details. Should he go through the whole thing? That would take time, as he was not the world's fastest reader. Was it time that Selma had? If he did not read the whole thing, would he be missing clues about this Rose Devil and his relationship to Allen Lang? Probably, but were they of dire import? Possibly not.

And where the hell *was* Selma?
In hiding. She must be.
"Selma," he whispered, "keep your head down. I'm coming."

Chapter Four

1974

Chuck brought Selma to the bus station, bought her a ticket back to Pennsylvania, and sat with her, waiting for the bus to be start accepting passengers. After a nearly silent morning—at breakfast, she offered nothing more than a subvocalized response to both Chuck's "Good morning" greeting and his "How did you sleep?" query—Selma broke the moratorium on speech.

She asked: "So, where are you going next?"

"Reno," he said. "Maybe San Diego. I'm getting my itinerary dates confused just now."

"Pretty exciting, huh?"

"It's a consultation gig," he said, shifting uncomfortably. "I go somewhere, I get paid to look at specs and tell someone in power all the flaws in the project. Then, I propose solutions, trying to make my company look like we know what the hell we're doing. That's kind of nice, if repetitive. The other junkets are tech courses and training crapola. Meetings and people bitching about why we can't make more money, get higher profile clients, that sort of thing. I suppose someone's making Action Plans for the company to follow, but that's not me. I just go where they say and do what I'm supposed to do. Part salesman, part logician, part bullshit artist."

She smiled at that. "You can talk a pretty line of shit when you want."

"Thanks," he said, trying to keep his tone neutral. "Was that an insult?"

When she looked at him, he saw more than a little mischief in her eyes, the slight curl of a smile, the glow in her cheeks. *Maaaaaybe*, that expression communicated, while her lips said, "Nope, just a statement of fact."

The bus station personnel announced that it was time for the departing folk to start making their way to the bus. "I guess that's my cue," she said.

"You want to give me a heads up the next time you come to visit?"

"Sure, Unk."

"Unk, huh?" Chuck had used this phrase in the military as an abbreviation for "unknowns," often in relationship to enemy maneuvers. He wasn't so sure he enjoyed being called such a thing himself.

"Kinda silly, huh?"

He did not respond. If she was feeling contrary, and he showed his disapproval, then she would simply continue to use the damned nickname. If he showed approval he did not feel, she would undoubtedly pick up on that, too. No, best to ignore it altogether.

"You going to be warm enough?"

"I stayed warm all the way here, I'll be fine all the way back."

"If you say so."

She opened her mouth to say something more, but then thought better of it. Closed her lips and held up one hand. Her wave was a curl of her fingers and a prim smile.

He grabbed her in a hug and kissed her forehead. "You be good, now. Okay?"

"Nah, Uncle Chuck," she said, "the trick is not getting caught."

He snickered at that one, and she laughed. "Yeah, well, then don't get caught."

She got onto the bus, found a window seat and looked down at him. Again, she gave him the curled finger wave, and he gave it right back. As the brakes hissed off, and the bus started moving, he realized her smile was gone, a frown replacing it.

On the way home, he realized he should really call Bea to let her know that Selma was on the way back. When he got home and did just that, Bea turned out to be quite frantic.

"Chuck, thank God, I've been calling for you, but you must've been on one of your trips."

"I—"

"She's gone, Chuck. Selma just left. Vanished."

"She's okay. I put her on a bus back home not an hour ago."

On Bea's end of the line, the breathing grew heavy, angry. "She's been with you all week and you decide to call me now?"

All *week*? Chuck felt his palms grow a layer of sweat. He had only gotten back to New York last night after five days in Baltimore . . . How long had she been prowling around his neighborhood? What had she seen, done, been exposed to . . .? Jesus. Why hadn't she said anything?

"*Chuck*?"

"She needed time. A little time away."

"I've been worried, Chuck. God, I've been—"

"Bea, she's on her way home, now."

"Thank God for his wisdom, mercy and generosity," Bea said, breathing a little more regularly. "Thank you Jesus. Amen."

"Amen," Chuck said, though the word was hollow as ever.

#

1977

Two phone calls. Chuck started with the more difficult of the two, a call to Bea. The line was scratchy, interference from distance or the elements, who could say? When Bea picked up, the connection proved disastrously weak. Bea's voice was an old woman's or a specter's. Or an old specter's voice.

"Yes?"

"Bea, it's Chuck. I'm in Los Angeles."

"Oh, Chuck. Praise God, it's you. How is she? Has she been with that boy?"

Chuck had been silently arguing with himself about exactly what he should say to her. He had even debated lying, if only to keep her nerves calm. In the end, he decided on a policy of truth.

"I've been to her apartment. She wasn't in. Her neighbor had not seen her in a couple of days."

"What about her boyfriend? This Allen, character?"

"Well, I don't have an address for him. A full name either. I can say that she's connected to an Allen Lang—"

"That's his name. Lang. She did mention it once. She joked that it was 'a langshot' that a man like him would see a girl like her. A langshot, she said. You know, playing on 'a longshot'?"

"Yeah," Chuck said, "I gathered as much."

"Although I have no idea what she meant by that. 'A girl like me'? What kind of girl does she think she is?"

A valid question. "I honestly can't say because I don't know, Bea."

"I raised her," Bea said, "to be a good girl. A smart girl. A Christian girl."

"And I hope she's not mixed up with Allen Lang," Chuck said.

"Why not?"

And here it was, the moment of truth. Despite his resolution to be straight, Chuck nursed his doubts. If he should he come clean with all he had learned and experienced, what good would that do? In fact, it might do more harm than good, might'n't it? Should he spare her the worst of it? Hellfire . . . "Because it looks like this Allen Lang character is trouble."

"A troublemaker?"

"Yeah, and more than just the type who steals STOP signs on a Saturday night."

She took in air, as though this crime appeared on the ranking of Evil as directly comparable to, say, stealing a first born child. While such an act was technically larceny, Chuck had done similar stupid things as a teenager. He speculated Bea had, as well, but she had conveniently forgotten such things now that she was older and more certain of her place in Heaven. "Does he," she asked, "have a record?"

"I don't know," Chuck said, "but he's got something of a reputation."

Silence for a moment. "For what?"

"For a bunch of stupid things," Chuck said. "Things I hope Selma has not gotten herself mixed up in."

"She's a smart girl, Chuck. A real smart girl. I raised her to be moral and wise. I . . . Oh God, Chuck. I just want my baby to be all right. I want . . ." She started sobbing. "I knew I shouldn't have let her move out there. Not to California. Not three time zones away, she's too *far*. My heart, it can't reach that far. My hands can't reach. Chuck, I . . . Oh, Jesus, don't let my baby be hurt. Scared and alone in a terrifying world." Sobs gave way to a full cry, as words finally surrendered to a low moan of deepest misery.

He adopted a soothing voice. "Bea, c'mon. I'm sure she is all right. Just a little misguided right now, following her heart when her head's telling her the right way to go. She's . . . She's fine."

"How do you know, Chuck?" So far and so old, the line now made Bea into a bansidhe.

"Because I . . ." How *did* he know? Why did he believe she was hiding and well, when The Rose Devil's trail was one littered with corpses and crime? When Allen Lang was undoubtedly no better? "Because I've got faith," he said. "Where's yours?"

A sharp slap to the face could not have quieted Bea down any faster. "I— Oh, God, Chuck, I'm just so blasted *worried*. You don't have a child, you can't know what a mother feels . . . when her baby is gone."

I have more of an idea than you might expect. "That may be true," he said, "but I'm going to find her."

"And bring her home?"

"And make sure she's safe. If she's safe out here and wants to stay, who am I to stand in the way of her schooling?"

"No, no, *no*," Bea sounded on the verge of a tantrum. "She has to come home. You must make her realize—"

"I have to do nothing of the sort. I can only make sure she's safe. The decision is her's. She's practically an adult, now, Bea. She's earned our trust—"

"Not if she's dating a troublemaker!"

"Bea."

"Chuck."

Silence. Neither of the speakers wanted to give the other the satisfaction of saying they had been wrong.

Chuck finally broke the silence and avoided the topic. "I'll do what I can, Bea."

"Do you," Bea's made a sound like she wet her lips. "Do you *swear*?"

No pause for consideration; he'd already done the swearing to an empty apartment, a notebook, a plastic baggie of keys, and a good luck charm named Mr. Hands. "Yes, Bea. I swear to find her. To make her as safe as is humanly possible."

Silence, again. Finally, the ghostly voice said, "I can ask nothing more of you."

"I have to go," he said.

"Good luck, Chuck."

"Thanks, Bea."

"God bless and keep you."

"I'll call back, soon."

When he hung up the phone, the weight of black moods and thoughts dropped onto his shoulders and heart. What had he done? What promise had he just made?

"Hellfires," he muttered.

What if, as Bea feared, Selma truly was dead? He knew enough to say he would feel no differently. They shared no supernatural, ephemeral bond. His goddaughter could very well be lying in the ground somewhere, or fed to pigs, or her ashes scattered to the winds.

He shivered.

No. There was no time for him to think as much. Thinking like that was accepting defeat. He had only just begun looking for her. Besides, he realized the actual promise was only to find her.

Hopefully the search won't lead to a grave . . .

He picked up the phone again, and dialed a distance even longer than he already had. This time to Massachusetts. On the third ring, a woman answered, her voice slow and weary, trying to play at being chipper. "Wachusett Steel and Dye."

"Let me talk to Bernie."

Without a pause, she shut him down. "Mr. Wayne is in a meeting just now. Can I get your name and a message?"

"The name is Chuck Cave. The message is two words: Bacon Time."

"Pardon me, did you say 'Bacon time'?"

"Bacon time."

The line hissed as she considered this. In the background, he could hear the sounds of something scratching across paper, he hoped it was a pen and not her fingernail.

"Does he have your number?" This last came across as "*Ya numba*?" in case he'd forgotten he was calling New England. Chuck's lips stretched in a cockeyed grin.

"Nah, I'm out of town. The number is . . ." he recited the hotel's phone number. "I'm in Room 123."

"One, two, three," she said. "All right, Mr. Cave."

"Thanks, doll."

Her weary voice now found renewed strength, when she said, "Welcome, *honey*," saying this last like he was some kind of annoyance. He supposed he was.

#

1953

Bernard Wayne had only been a part of the 17th Infantry for less than a month, when Chuck took a liking to him. A smart fellow, funny when he tried, quiet the rest of the time. He looked like a high school quarterback and got cheesy crime paperbacks from stateside. He had cracked left incisor—due to an encounter, he claimed, with a mallet wielded by a girl's crazed brother—and eyes as blue as lightning.

He and Chuck would play cards with some of the others, and on the eve of April the 15th, a full day before the Reds would storm that little zit on the ass cheek of Korea, that the men called Pork Chop Hill, they were doing just that. Playing cards. After the fact reflection granted this game a nearly mythic resonance, a quality of capital-I-Importance: this simple game—in which Chuck would lose twenty bucks, and Bernie would rake in the pot, guffawing like some cartoon character "Haw, Haw, Haw"—posed the last quiet moment before the storm to come.

"You looking forward to getting home?" Bernie asked, and if a listener had not known beforehand that he was green, that question would have nailed any lingering uncertainties.

The way the other players looked at him, he must've felt sheepish. He was silent for almost three seconds before unleashing that guffaw—a little too late—and pulling the old "Of course, of course. What I meant was, what are you most looking forward to?"

The fellows grunted at this, letting the kid wipe at that egg he'd splashed on his face.

Dwight, immediately on the kid's right, answered first: "I miss my Bea. She's been my girl since high school. We got married before I come here. I left, she had our little chap Nick in the oven. Can't wait to see the both of 'em."

"Kids? No way do I want to get settled down," Delano Mortagne said. He was a smooth talker, born with brown eyes so that the unwary might have a chance to notice he talked a lot of shit and a smile that could disarm a Russian Premier's bodyguard. He was also a confirmed woman hound, and his answer of "I want to chase a little tail that speaks English good," came as a surprise to no one.

Monty 's eyes got kind of wet, and his cheeks turned the color of sunset, when he said, "Ah hell, boys. I miss the big Lone Star. Miss my family's rose fields. I mean, working them, that's hell and hard as anything. Whenever I was out there, budding or doing sticks or . . . Hell, I wanted to be any-damn-where's else but those fields. Now? I'd give a month's pay just to see them again. Shoot. Chuck knows all about 'em."

Curious eyes turned Chuck's way. He nodded, as though admitting to something as embarrassing as whacking off. "Yeah, yeah. Looks like when I get stateside, I'll be visiting the Texas badlands and seeing these fields for myself. He won a bet."

Monty waggled his eyebrows at this, and the fellas all laughed. No one bothered to ask just what they'd wagered on, but Monty said, "We grow *everything* bigger in Texas."

"So, what you looking forward to, Chuck?" Bernie asked.

"You know, I'll tell you," Chuck offered a smile, "There just is not a single good piece of steak in this entire damned country? I want something just introduced to the bar-b-que. On it long enough to say hi-how-are-ya and then on the plate. Inch thick and juicy. Medium rare, seasoned like my dad does. Yeah. The kind you can take a big old bite of, and have the juices squirt down your throat. Slice of heaven is a steak. Yeah."

"You ain't never had a steak, 'til you've had one in Texas," Monty said, but he said something similar about beer, bar-b-que, brisket, and pussy.

"Can one state hold up so much of the bar of quality?" Chuck asked, "I have my doubts."

"Cowboys don't lie," Monty said.

"They just improve the truth," Delano said, and everyone laughed.

"How about you, Bernie? What're you looking forward to?"

He laughed, and it was a sorrow filled sound. "This'll probably come as a surprise," he said, "but everything I've ever wanted, I've got here. Some good chums, a deck of cards to pass the time, some brews. Gimme a Sox game on the radio, I'm set."

"That's because you're green," Delano said.

"So you say," Bernie said, still smiling. "When I go home, I've got a steel businessman's shoes to fill. Nice pay, but a lousy job. Dad's been grooming me for the position since I was seven. This late in the game, I ain't got no choice but to do it."

Chuck looked into his face. "You're aren't even twenty-one, are you?"

"Only just," Bernie said, "and everything's already decided."

After almost two minutes, Monty said, "Fold," and the game was pretty much over.

The next day, the Reds invaded Pork Chop Hill. During the three days of Hell, Delano would lose an eye, Bernie would catch a burst across his ass cheeks, and Chuck would take one in his shoulder pulling Bernie to safety inside a mostly compromised, but still partially serviceable bunker.

As Chuck laid down fire at the Enemy, and Monty did what he could to treat the wounds, Bernie sputtered and spat about his Daddy's business, crying all the while. Chuck got so fed up, he snapped, "Just tell your Daddy, 'No' and don't become the businessman."

In the little quiet to come, he checked on Bernie, who was still weeping—from the pain or his own future, Chuck could not say for sure—but before Chuck could say something, Bernie said "You saved my bacon, Chuck. Jesus, but you done. If you ever need me, Chuck. If it's ever your bacon time, all you do is call me. Whatever I'm doing, it'll wait. You saved my bacon, Chuck. You saved my bacon."

At the time, Chuck had only shook his head. "I didn't do nothing special," he said, "You'd of done the same."

Bernie wasn't listening to him, though. He was lost somewhere else.

#

1977

Chuck began to wonder if that vow had been only the words of a wounded man when, ten minutes later, the phone rang.

"Cave," he said.

Bernie was on the line: "I would've called earlier, but that woman doesn't deliver messages very quickly." Chuck could hear the frown in his voice.

Here is was, over twenty years after the Hill, and Bernard Wayne still sounded pretty much the same. Voice maybe a little rougher from the cigarettes, a little more of those Bah-ston traits the guys had razzed him about, but otherwise essentially the same as it had been, Hellfire: twenty damn years ago . . .

"Where are you," Bernie asked, "and when do you need me?"

Chuck could not repress a smile of relief. It lightened his words. "I'm in Los Angeles."

"Long distance, huh?"

"Yeah."

"And when do you need me?"

As simple as that. No questions about what Chuck had been up to, no uncertainty about being able to get away from the day job, no forgetfulness about promises made—although promises on a battlefield carry a certain weight that even the most "absent minded" can never truly forget. Bernie was a good man, a great friend. When was the last time they'd spoken? Sometime during the late fifties? Wow, had it been that long ago? Chuck felt a shiver, had it been over fifteen years?

Chuck said, "When you can get away."

"Pressing?"

"Yes, but not critical."

"Then I'll leave this afternoon. Catch whatever flight I can. Haven't seen California in a dog's age, and LA never."

"You been out here much? Know the scene?"

Bernie laughed. "If by 'the scene' you mean a beach and a resort hotel, then yeah I know it. Anything you can tell me about the caper?"

Caper. He made it sound somehow romantic and dangerous, when only the second part of that summary was immediately true. "My god daughter came out here for school. Dwight's girl."

"Dwight? Didn't he—"

"Yeah," Chuck said. "The tumors did what the commies' bullets never could." The air felt somehow cold, now, as he reflected on this. "He never saw her, but he asked me on his death bed if I'd take care of her. Keep an eye on her. That sort of thing."

"Play Daddy?"

Was that question carrying a little racy tete-a-tete? If so, then Bernie's deadpan was nigh impervious. Still, the question carried odd sensations and inferences. "More like keep her out of trouble."

"That's what I meant," Bernie said, as a matter of fact.

"Yeah," Chuck said, "well, Delano'd have a whole different take on things."

"Jesus, Delano Montagne . . ." Now that the business part was done, Bernie's voice softened, developed some nostalgia. "I wonder what the hell happened to him?"

"I saw him a couple years ago. He's on this coast, up in San Francisco. Married, if you can—"

Bernie laughed. "The old tail chaser's gotten himself civilized, huh? After all that protesting?" The sound of Bernie's laugh brought back memories of good times, and those not so good, but linked by deepest camaraderie. "I can't say that I'm surprised?"

"He's married to a girl young enough to be his granddaughter almost."

"Again, I'm not surprised. She must be some kind of desperate."

"Nah, she's a charmer. Sweetheart and a half. Hippie chick."

"Really?" The laughter vanished. In its place, a simmering anger. "Delano's gone flag burner?"

"Nope," Chuck said. "Sunbeam's all right. One in a billion, maybe. Delano's a lucky guy."

"Did you say Sunbeam?"

"The girl's name. For once, those hippie names fits. She's a peach." *A little bruised now*, he thought, *but no less sweet*.

"You feeling like you're missing out?"

Chuck's mouth played with a smile but lost it before long. "So, give me a call when you get the flight information. I'll meet you at the airport."

"Will do," Bernie said. "Lucky me has a travel agent on retainer, here at the office."

"Lucky you."

"Over and out," Bernie said.

They hung up, and Chuck tried to distract himself by reading through the notebook for an hour. Then, he slid it under the mattress, along with the parcel of drugs, and went down to the hotel restaurant and ordered a steak. Funny thing: as delicious as the meal idea was, and though the restaurant was filled with the most mouth-watering aromas, the steak itself was nothing better than edible. A let down.

By the time he got back to the room, a message awaited him. Bernie was coming in on the ten-thirty from Boston.

Chapter Five

1962

Chuck stood among the rolling, pleasantly landscaped hills serving as homes for the cold, gray headstones. He did his damnedest to stand tall and strong next Bea, who could not have been any more blind. Her hands kept busy, one using Chuck's handkerchief to catch her sorrow, while the other held the hand of their three year old child in such a death grip that little Selma asked, on several occasions, "Not so hard, mommy. You're holding me too tight." However, this plea came as little more than a whisper, far too soft for Bea to hear, not with all that sobbing.

Chuck leaned close, "Don't squeeze the life out of your child's hand." As soon as he said this, he regretted it. A little too callow for such an environment. But the day itself was heartless . . . The sun shone lemon yellow among the few puffy white clouds and brilliant blue sky, the wind frolicked between the graves and four pall bearers, as they carried the terribly small coffin and laid it to rest in a hole near his father.

As soon as she saw the lustrous gray of the coffin's lid, Bea's wailed grew throaty and then hoarse.

The priest's words delivered little comfort, and the piteous glares of folks Chuck either knew only from family photos or not at all offered little better.

More than a few of those strangers' eyes held something approaching contempt. How, those eyes demanded, could Bea call herself a wife and mother, this woman who let first her husband and then her five year old son both find their way into the ground before her? Certainly this, those eyes continued, was the mark of the most egregious carelessness. And when those eyes turned toward little Selma, they held a horrified curiosity: What fate, they asked, awaits *you*?

Chuck felt the desire—the need, really—to punch their lights out. To shout in their faces. To sling spittle laced invectives their way. He held his tongue, however, and stewed.

The funeral passed, and Bea received verbal tokens of her family and friends' pity. When she got too antsy, Chuck led Selma away from this.

"How you doing, kiddo?" Chuck asked, and she shrugged.

They walked past the grave, and she maintained a steady pace, making no effort to hurry or pause at either her father or brother's resting place.

"Kind of hurts, huh?" he asked, and she nodded.

"Will I be put here, too?"

Chuck felt a wholly different wind pass through him. "You don't have to worry about that for a long, long time . . ."

"But will I end up here, too?" She looked around the graveyard. "And Mommy?"

Chuck crouched beside her. His knees popped. Only three but Selma looked so grown up, wearing a black dress and shoes, and terribly bright blue socks. Her hair had come free of the carefully applied clips, and now hung limp around her shoulders. Her face was empty of emotion. Chuck wondered if this was normal.

"Well, people all die," Chuck said.

Selma looked into his eyes, and now he saw something shimmering in her baby blues. Tears, like diamonds, precious from their scarcity. A fat one rolled down her cheek. "And everyone gets put in the ground?"

"Not everyone," Chuck said. "Some people ask for cremation."

"What's that?"

"Well, that's when the body is, uhm, incinerated."

"What's that?" she asked, that relentless mind of hers.

"A person can ask that their body be burned," Chuck said, "The ashes can be put in a special jar, called an urn, and saved. Or those ashes can be scattered."

"Scattered?"

Chuck waved his hand through the air as though casting sand. "Sprinkled, sort of. Some of it gets carried by the wind."

"And the rest?"

"Well, if a person wants their ashes scattered, they'll usually leave instructions to do so over a special place."

"Like the backyard? By the spruce trees?"

Chuck smiled as he considered this, and Selma developed her "Are you poking fun at me?" frown. He quickly dissuaded her retaliatory expression with complete, consummate agreement. "Yep. Like the back yard by the spruce trees."

"How do you know?" Selma asked.

"How do I know what?"

"What a person wants? To be stuck underground or burned all up? How do they tell you, when they're dead?"

"They don't tell you when they're dead. Usually a person gets to thinking about it, while they're alive. They write this stuff down. What they write is called a Last Will."

"Last Will what?"

"Last Will and Testament."

"Testament?"

"A long name for 'Final Wishes'."

"Oh." She glanced at the grass around her shoes. "Did Nicky make a Last Will and Testama?"

"No," Chuck said. "I don't know that he really had much of a chance to think about this stuff."

"*So they just stuck him in the ground*? Even though he was scared of it? Of the dark? Of tiny spaces? He couldn't even stay under the basement stairs for more than a minute without screaming, he . . . I don't think he wants to be down there. I . . . I just don't think so."

"Well, your mom decided that he would."

"And 'cuz he don't have no Last Will and . . . Well, he din't have no Last Will they just done what *she* says?"

Chuck felt this sliding into a place that was even more uncomfortable than it already was. He decided not to answer that question. "But that box you saw, Nicky's not really in there anymore."

"But he is," she said. "I saw him."

"You saw his . . . body. But that's not him. What made him Nicky, that's gone away."

"To Heaven?"

Chuck pursed his lips. He'd stumbled into yet another awful topic of conversation.

"Mom says he's in Heaven with Daddy."

"Your Mom's a pretty smart gal," Chuck said.

Another tear fell down her cheek.

"You cry if you want, okay?" Chuck said.

"You aren't."

"I cried on the plane ride out. I'm trying to be strong for you and your mom."

"Why?"

"Because sometimes people need someone to hang onto."

"But Mommy's way over there."

"Not literally," Chuck said, "but . . . well, sometimes it's literally. Sometimes they just need someone around to be strong, so they can feel safe while they aren't so strong."

"Is that how my Daddy was? Strong? Did Mommy and Nicky hang onto him?"

"Your Daddy was one of the strongest men I ever knew."

"Did you cry when . . . when he got putted in the ground?"

Chuck nodded.

"Who was strong for you?"

"A friend of mine. And a friend of your Daddy's." Chuck thought about Bernard Wayne's quiet and calming presence. He would have to drop by Boston and visit, one of these days. Maybe in a couple months?

More tears fell, and Selma held out her hands for a hug. "I need," she said between sobs, "someone to hang on."

Chuck pulled her into his arms, and she clung around his neck tight, as her body heaved with the sobs. He said nothing, just petted her hair and held her tight.

#

1977

When Bernie emerged from the plane, Chuck did not recognize him. Maybe it was the facial hair, a thick beard peppered with silver hairs, or the hair line that had receded enough to bare his entire crown, or the lines on his face, or the slight bulge to his gut. His posture was ramrod straight and tall, his arms powerful under a Hawaiian shirt. His gray eyes remained hidden behind a pair of sunglasses, and he slung a bag across his shoulder.

Then, Bernie said, "Chuck Cave," and his lips split in that all too familiar, ragged grin, "as I live and breathe. You haven't

50

changed at all." The Boston accent made this sound something like *'Yew hahn't changed a ahl.'*

They clasped hands and Bernie's grip was tighter than ever before. His left ring finger featured a band of gold.

"You have," Chuck said. "I didn't recognize you."

"I'm ageing gracelessly," he said, and rubbed a hand across his gleaming scalp. "Started going bald back in 63, and then stopped around 71. Holding the line, these days."

"Let's get your luggage."

"Done and done," Bernie said, hefting the strap off his shoulder. "I pack light."

"The doll in your life pack heavy?"

Bernie's eyebrow raised with more than a little confusion.

"When a man gets caged by a doll, she usually leaves a ringer." Chuck indicated the gold ring on Bernie's finger with a nod. "You've been marked, my friend. Tagged as wed and off limits to any and all applicants."

Bernie twirled it, straight faced, but his eyes got a little misty. "Yeah, I got tagged all right, and yeah, whenever we'd travel, Margie would always pack too much."

Chuck noticed the past tense and did not inquire further. Bernie answered the question anyway. "Car wreck took her from me. A couple of hippie kids, who walked away with scratches, plowed into the driver's side of her car."

"I'm sorry," Chuck said.

"Yeah," Bernie said. "Let's hit a bar, chew the fat. You still need to tell me the op."

First a caper, now an op. Chuck shook his head and clapped his buddy on the arm. "Right this way."

#

The airport watering hole proved to be a bar in name alone. Too brightly lit, too much ventilation, very little privacy. The real gin joint was only a five minute drive. The place was named Lucille's Suds, and an old black man owned it. He was maybe fifty, with a paunch and a distinct resemblance to BB King. Chuck did not comment about this, as he was certain the man must've heard plenty of jokers saying the same thing, while believing themselves to be original.

Bernie swallowed two ryes in less than twenty seconds and then ordered soda water. Chuck had a beer, and nursed it.

Bernie started the ball rolling. "So, Dwight's girl came out this way."

"Yeah. And she got herself missing."

"Missing?"

Chuck nodded.

"She's how old now?"

"Eighteen," Chuck said.

"Boyfriend?"

"Some joker called Allen. If that's the same 'Allen' I've been hearing about, then this joker is bad news."

"How bad?"

Chuck leaned conspiratorially close. "I found a brick of dope stashed in her apartment, and some kind of manifesto. Not counterculture, this is deep underground crap."

"Jesus," Bernie said. "*Bad*, bad news. 'Zat why you aren't going to the cops?"

Chuck rubbed his palm across the whiskers on his chin. "I probably should. I know what you're thinking. Yeah, I probably should."

"But you aren't," Bernie said, "and there's got to be a reason."

"I know her. Been seeing her all her life," Chuck said. "Nothing I've ever seen of her would fit her into this little setup. The bad boyfriend? Sure. But drugs? No way. Not Selma Kowalski . . . Not Dwight Kowalski's little girl."

"There're a lot of parents use the same line," Bernie said. "'Not my kid, not my kid.' Sometimes you don't know a person like you think."

"Sometimes," Chuck nodded, "but not this time. Anyway, I promised Dwight. And there's more."

"More?"

"Someone's trying to kill her."

Bernie sat rock still. Chuck took a sip of the beer. "Two groups. One pro, one definitely not."

"Military?"

Chuck considered this. "Maybe some training for the pro group. Not on your life for the others."

Bernie gestured for Chuck to go on, before taking a hit off his effervescing, soda water.

"Two sets of gunmen showed up at her place, while I was waiting," he recounted the situation with the two groups of shooters.

"That's what 'Max' called them? 'The Devil's Boys'?" Bernie asked.

"Something like it."

Bernie's lips turned down, but fury filled his eyes. "Sounds like a God damned hippie name."

Chuck shook his head. "I don't think so."

"They got all those crazy names. Moonunit. Amadeaus Meteorhead. Devil could easily be—"

"I think the Rose Devil is someone else."

"Hold up, Sarge. Hold up." After a pause, Bernie asked, "Did you just say 'The Rose Devil'?"

"Yeah—"

Bernie guffawed, still sounding like a cartoon character, though age had made him a little rougher around the edges. "Oh, that's definitely a Hippie name."

Chuck recounted his search of Selma's apartment and a little more about what he had gleaned from the manifesto.

Bernie's guffaws dwindled and died off. Soon a melancholy touched his voice, "What the hell has Dwight's little girl gotten herself into?"

"I wonder the same thing," Chuck said. "And I need to find out. For Dwight. After I do, sure, I can go to the cops."

"If they aren't already after you," Bernie said, "who knows what kind of evidence you left at that shoot out."

Chuck pursed his lips. "I do a fair job of picking up after myself."

Bernie stared into Chuck's face for a full minute before Chuck finally met his eyes. Whatever the Massachusetts man found in those eyes made him tremble. "You mean . . . You've done this before? Been involved in shootouts? I mean, after the Hill. After that shit half a world away. You been seeing action *since then*."

"I've had few run ins," Chuck said, "with trouble, yeah."

"And you're running into it again?"

"I never start the fights," Chuck said, "but I end them. And I try not to break too many toes along the way. I still have a clear conscience." *Mostly.*

Bernie finished the soda water and ordered another rye.

"If you want to go—"

"I didn't figure you'd call in the Bacon Time for a game of pinochle," Bernie said. "I said I was there when you needed me. I'm here."

Chuck nodded. "Thanks."

"What's next?"

"A good question." Chuck considered this. "I've got a couple of avenues to pursue. I don't intend to put you in any danger. Mostly, I need someone to watch my back."

"Stop pussyfooting around, okay? I'm here," Bernie said. "Use me, or I'll get mad."

Chuck nodded, slapped the plastic baggie of keys on the bar. "What do you think these fit?"

"They look like door keys. A house, maybe? I dunno." Bernie picked the baggie up, scrutinizing it for a dozen seconds before his lips found the deepest frown yet. "Then again, there're keys in here that do more than open locks."

Now it was Chuck's turn to cock his eyebrow. He also cocked his head to the side. "Meaning?"

"There're more keys than you realize," Bernie said, shaking the bag. "See that white residue?"

The inside of the bottom seam was spotted with white specks. *Some kind of paint chips or sugar maybe?* Chuck said, "Yeah?"

Bernie's voice dropped to a coarse whisper. "That's cocaine, my friend."

"Hellfire."

Bernie nodded. "There's more going on in heaven and earth, Horatio . . ."

Chuck sucked in his lower lip. "What do you think?"

"Reefer *and* coke *and* gunmen? Two factions? You got yourself one hell of a fight on your hands. You think we can pull this off on our own?"

"I don't know who else to call," Chuck said. "Kind of down to the wire."

"Delano's out of the picture. Don't you know anyone else?"

"I know plenty of people, but none who might be able to help with *this*."

"All right," Bernie downed the soda water. "Instead of jerking off here, howsabout letting our soles slap some pavement?"

Chuck had to admit he was feeling a little antsy. "Yeah."

#

1957

Chuck woke up with the woman's arm across his chest. Dawn's sunlight made the thin window shade glow the yellow-brown of a healing bruise. His head swam a moment, not quite throbbing—he had not had *that* much to drink the night before, only a quartet of beers to wash down two shots of Cuervo—but still experiencing the morning after mental loop-de-loops.

Every few seconds produced a little more clarity, as though the dawn's light could somehow strip away the gauzy layers that sleep and liquor had laid over his mind. The room's ceiling featured circular designs from poor brush work, an effect that brought to mind his first bedroom; this ceiling, however, was mostly clear of the web of cracks found in his childhood home. And this was a dirty white, paint touched up by cigarette smoke and age.

Beside the bed, the clock rolled over to 7:05. In the corner, a few cardboard boxes with the top flaps open, waiting to be unpacked. His uniform hung in the closet, a clean and pressed ghost.

The woman shivered, offered a quiet moan, and then fell into placid snoring. In sleep, her pretty face took on an unencumbered quality. Softness. He looked at her, and tried to find a smile, but did not find a real one. Her name was Lucy. They were trying to make a go of it, but that, he felt, was done.

He recollected the previous evening's conversation, and the black mood returned.

"Don't go to bed angry," she had suggested, her doe eyes blinking too quickly, a sure sign that she was herself irate. "I understand why you don't—"

"Let's just stop talking about it," he'd said, and they had.

No sex. She had been having difficulty with that ever since Texas. Oh, the idea sounded all right, but when it came to the action, well . . . Not that he could blame her. There was only so much a human body and mind could withstand, and being trussed up by a trusted, authority figure and abused with a knife's edge in awful, awful ways was certainly the breaking point. Chuck did not press the issue, but the issue certainly weighed upon him. For good or ill, he was a man who liked sex.

No sex, but the talk of having . . . No, no. He had no time for that sort of thing, not that it could come about short of the some kind of immaculate conception. He reached over to the nightstand, to the pack of cigarettes and the matchbook, lit one and took a drag.

The smoke curled through the air, and he exhaled as quickly as he'd inhaled. Hellfire, this brand tasted awful. He stubbed it out, then regretted not taking another pull or two.

She shifted beside him. Started to drag her way out of dream. Pretty face, slender body. The sheet held most of the scars she had carried out of Texas. The white linen fell over her form, emphasizing the swell of her breasts and hips, her slender legs. Her brunette hair fell across the pillows like a fan.

"Morning," she said, her voice a drawl that no longer brought an affectionate smile to his lips.

"Morning."

"Can I have a drag?"

"I just finished it."

"Ah."

He considered those boxes in the corner, the top one with its flaps open and red fabric draped over one side. They could be filled with clothes, bedroom dressings, or the few items of country kitch she'd brought along. Little piles of those boxes were scattered around the tiny house.

"You're still angry."

He considered this, apparently taking too long because she spoke again before he could answer her.

"Chuck? We don't have to— Let's not talk about it, okay? Let's not be angry this morning."

"You want eggs?" he asked, but there was a hardness to his voice that would make even the firmest egg seem runny.

"I— You want I should make pancakes?"

"I want . . ." In that moment, he decided he was not hungry at all. "I want coffee."

Dust motes drifted in the morning sunshine. She said, "Oh."

He slid from beneath her arm and out the bed and walked across the room, never once looking back, and out the door. He moved with the same stiffness that he would later, when he carried the valise at his side and the uniform across his shoulder.

He knew her to be watching him, knew her green eyes to be watery. Should his own not be? Yet, they were not. Outside the kitchen, down a short hallway and a right hand turn brought him to the small kitchen. Cozy, the rental agent had described it, but now it felt confining. He opened the coffee, smelled the grounds, but still could not smile. The black mood weighed upon his soul like iron ingots.

"Chuck?" Lucy stood at the doorway, wearing a white robe over her nightgown.

"Mmmm?"

"You want pancakes?"

"No."

"Eggs?"

"No."

"Ah."

He scooped the grounds into the filter, inserted this into the coffeemaker, and then added some hot water.

She said, "Isn't that a bit much for so little water?"

"I like it strong. You know that."

Lucy's hand—not the one holding her against the doorjamb, but the one left flying without a purpose—moved down and stopped atop her firm belly. "You could make it as strong as you want," she said.

"I could."

"I—"

"I thought," he said, "you didn't want to talk about it, anymore."

"Here it is, Sunday morning," she said, trying to sound cheerful, but the perkiness she adopted could not convince a clown to smile. "It's a bright, wide-open day. What would you like to do with it?"

He thought about this for a moment before answering, "Maybe go for a drive."

The cheer vanished, and her eyes filled with water, again. "Ah. A drive? Sounds nice."

"Mmmm."

She across the kitchen and into the breakfast nook, sat down at the table. Soon, the smell of coffee filled the kitchen, creeping into the nook on cat's feet. Chuck filled one mug and then a second. Added creamer and sugars, walked the mugs across to the nook and found Lucy sobbing into her elbow. When she sensed his presence, she wiped the tears away and put her sob-damp rendition of a happy face back on. Now, she looked like a clown herself. An empty smile painted on her lips, not at all reflected in her miserable eyes.

He held out a mug for her, and she took it, sipped it. Her voice warbled when she said, "It's strong."

"How I like it." Those words tasted awful as they slipped off his tongue. "Strong is good."

"Can I say anything?" she said.

"Say whatever you like," Chuck said, but she did not.

"You don't want any?"

He looked at his coffee and took a sip. "About what we were speaking of last night?"

She nodded, quick and shallow.

"I said I didn't, and I don't," he said.

"Not ever?"

He shook his head, firm negation.

"I . . . I can live without, too. For you. I . . ."

"No," he said, and this was the first real compassion he'd showed all morning. "I don't think you can."

"Chuck—"

"But I can't have them. I won't. Running around and getting into . . . Can't you see I can't?"

"But—"

"Drink your coffee, dear."

And like that, they were no longer giving it a try.

#

1977

Swarms of young men and women buzzed around the Cathay Roller Rink, and when Chuck and Bernie entered, all the closest eyes turned onto them like a microscope's light targeting a particularly ugly specimen of bacteria. The place was a good hundred feet wide and twice as deep, much of this dominated by the eponymous rink, where even now close to forty teens zipped round and round, their wheels grinding against the scuffed hardwood. Around this rink stood tables and stools and kids with sneers and hand rolled cigarettes, choking smoke hanging in the air sweet and bitter at once. Loudspeakers near a record setup blared some kind of bouncing music, the vapid stuff, a perfect fit for the "sport" these kids pursued.

As the men moved among them, more eyes found them—glares so mean that, were they flesh, they might snap at the men as they walked by, gouge out some skin or muscle, chew them up, swallow them.

"Feeling like an outsider?" Bernie asked.

Chuck merely grunted, and continued to move among them. When the young saw that these fellows did not wear uniforms or carry badges, most of them went back to what they were doing—as far as Chuck could tell, this was finding new and unusual ways to waste time. The record changed, though the quality of sound did not improve, before Chuck found the faces he was looking for.

The twenty year old had a rugged physique, a scruffy chin, hair hanging ragged and dirty down to his shoulders, eyes glazed with the smoke and chemical aids, and he wore the same denim rags Chuck had last seen him in, one day filthier.

"Your name's Dexter, right?" Chuck asked.

The boy stared at him with a mix of surprise, disgust and apathy. His retinue of lost boys and girls were diminished from yesterday's horde. Perhaps they milled around the rest of these masses. Dexter asked, "I know you, pops?"

"You called me a panty sniffer," Chuck said, "when I was walking around 'your neighborhood' yesterday."

Dexter's mouth opened with a monosyllabic "yaaaaaa" of recognition. His eyes, however, did not reflect the relaxed grin. They were too busy taking in both Chuck and Bernie, who was ostensibly looking away and around, but still cut an intimidating figure. "You cops."

"Nope," Chuck said. "Let's take a walk."

"Why?"

"Because I say 'please'?"

"And I," Bernie said, leaning in close and fast, "break skulls."

That he was surrounded by his buddies did not seem to provide much relief for Dexter. Sweat rolled down his face and exposed chest, making the brown curliques of hair on that chest gleam in the whirling lights. "Sure, man. Let's. Let's take some air, huh?" To his buddies, Dexter said, "I'm gonna take some air—" But they were already gone.

What loyal company you keep, Dexter, Chuck thought.

"You skate?" Dexter asked, as Chuck maneuvered him toward the front doors. After a breath, Dexter said, "No, huh? Well, neither do—" He broke into a run through the crowd. "*Narcs, man! Narcs!*" and all hell broke loose.

Chapter Six

June 5th, 1977

Selma was not the first person to cross the stage, nor the last. Not with a name like Kowalski. She was stuck right in the middle, and with nearly two hundred kids that meant a long wait. Still, Chuck did not get terribly antsy, until the high school principal—a dumpy looking man in horn rimmed glasses with an unfortunately, pronounced lisp—announced, "Thelma Kowalthki," then he drowned out even Bea's applause with his own.

She crossed the stage with pride, tall and pretty, possessing both grace and presence, received that diploma case in her left hand, shook the principal's outstretched paw with her right, and offered a pearly white smile. Then, she was done, her gown rippled as she made her way down the stairs and into one of the middle rows of folding chairs, amongst her friends and classmates, giggling at the principals' pronunciations through the rest of the class list (particularly for a poor young dear named Sissy Tassing-Smythe), and reveling in the celebration of their accomplishment.

More bodies followed the lisped beckons, and applause came from both the audience of pride puffed parents as well as the students themselves, congratulating each other on a job well done.

She's really gone and done it, he thought. She's a big girl, now. A young woman. When in hellfire did she go and do that?

He realized he said this last aloud when Bea turned her worried eyes and o-shaped mouth toward him before asking, "Go and do what? Are you talking about Selma?"

"She got big," he said.

"They do that." Bea's o-shape spread into a grin. "Kids, I mean."

"But it seems like only yesterday, you two came out to The City for a visit."

"Why do you call it that?" Bea asked. "There are plenty of cities, you know."

"Plenty of others, but not a one of them is quite like that beast," Chuck said.

"I suppose."

The principal chastised a trio of young men for launching and maintaining a beach ball in the air over the gathered young people. The students tittered, and the gathered parents offered sympathetic groans. Principal Sylvester the Cat was far too uptight for such a time of celebration, Chuck thought, let them play today, for tomorrow the real world began . . .

The principal raised a hand to his tassel and asked the students to do likewise. "Ath you move from thith, your career as thudenths, entering the world before you, ath you move from thchool to life, tho thall you move the tathle from left to wight." He raised the tassle, passed the cord over the forward pointing corner of the mortarboard, and then smiled. "Congratulathionth, Clath of Nineteen-Theventy-Theven," and those ticking time bombs in the folding chairs, that quiet, waiting mass of young people in blue gowns erupted into sound and motion, filling the air with screams of delight, hoots, and hundreds of spinning, blue squares. Hats no more, these were now Frisbees, twirling and whirring through the air, the bi colored tassles wriggling out of control and dragging them off course. Headgear had become a fleet of drunken UFOs.

Lads and lasses jumped up from their seats. Boys clapped one another on the back, girls embraced, and all the sexes shivered with excitement. Soon, the band played its powerful, mostly in-tune exuent music, and teachers clapped their hands for attention. The students would not have it. They broke ranks, moving as they pleased, all in the general expected direction, but not at all in an orderly fashion.

I'd hate, Chuck thought, *to be in the middle of that chaos.* It looked worse than combat.

#

1977

Narcs, man! Narcs! Once released, these words spread like fire, burning down the marginal holds on the chaos in the room. In the breath between the first repetition and the second, the panic it caused grew well beyond the confines of anyone's control.

Terrified bodies stormed toward the exits, shoving anyone in the way down and out. Stampeding animals showed more courtesy, and in that instant Dexter had more opportunities to vanish than he probably knew what to do with. He ducked low and moved fast, and within seconds, he was one body amongst the shuffle of kings, queens, jacks and deuces, an all but invisible member of the lost boys and girls. Gone, baby, gone . . .

Not everyone was going in the opposite direction. A quartet of toughs—wearing dirty, ripped denim vests and headbands, red gang colors on their arms—came toward them, leering like predators as they pulled weapons from their pockets—a Batangas knife, a pair of nunchucks, a zip gun, and the most powerful weapon of the lot, a .25 caliber Saturday night special. Gang kids.

"Now wait," Chuck said, but the quartet did not. They came forward in a flash, but they did not move as a unit. They practically shoved each other aside in an effort to get blooded on these narcs.

The knife blade flashed toward Bernie, but he caught the wielder's wrist and twisted. Bone broke, and the weapon hit the floor a second before its owner.

The nunchucks man flipped the deadly wooden shafts through the air with a wild glee, lashing them at Chuck's face with irregular attacks. Chuck dodged once, twice, again.

The kid with his zip gun—a unique composite of a coffee pot percolator tube-rod fitted on a wooden block grip—sited and sneered as he fired, that sneer vanished when the weapon exploded with his hand.

The black with the Saturday night special kept trying for a good shot at Chuck, but Chuck made sure to keep the nunchucks man in the way.

Another volley of flashy attacks came, and Chuck ducked and dodged, catching glancing blows across the forehead and shoulder, before his fist found the kid's throat and punched his adam's apple. The kid ate floor, clearing the way for the Saturday night special, whose owner grinned like an idiot as he aimed. "Dead to rights, baby," he whispered.

He didn't spot Bernie until the foot kicked the pistol ceilingward, and the round discharged harmlessly overhead. By the time, the black tough had regained his senses, Chuck had pulled his own weapon, so much larger than the .25 caliber pea shooter.

"Run," Chuck said, and the boy did, joining the mass.

"Dexter's gone, Chuck."

And so he was, until Chuck aimed the .45 for the ceiling and squeezed the trigger three times.

Flash cracks. Chuck was surprised how audible the .45 was over the cacophony of terror. Not the thunder of a shotgun, not the deafening rat-a-tat-tat of a fully automatic submachine gun in an apartment building's hallway, but the pistol still made quite a presence.

At the first shot, many of the people within spitting distance of Chuck immediately dropped to the floor. On the second, a dozen more people, a ring beyond those already covering their heads joined their friends on the floor. At the third, still more. Screams of "Narcs!" and "Raid!" changed to unintelligible whimpers. The time for stampeding had vanished. Berserk animals got sane enough to recall that living was better than any alternative.

Not Dexter, though. Of course, not him. To go down was to give up. No, he still sought escape. As though he might somehow get away. In response to Chuck's calls for him to "Hold it!" Dexter darted through hunkered and huddled people.

Bernie gave Chuck a crazy eyed look, a silent communication of outrage, "You brought a gun? Here? Fired it? *Here*?" and then ran after their target. Dexter neared the door with every heartbeat.

Chuck came along last, slow and careful, to keep the gun, which he now held pointed toward the floor, from accidentally murdering any one of the whimpering masses. They did not look up at him but burrowed beneath arms or hands, ostriches born from apes.

"Move," he said, "*move*." He could not put much force behind the words, they came out dull as a butter knife.

Ahead of them all, a bottleneck at the front doors. People hunkered low but remained intent on escape. Dexter found a fresh burst of speed when he arrived there. It must have been adrenaline that made him strong enough to yank the people out of his way. Girls and smaller boys flew around him, shoved aside and back, like human shields.

Chuck silently cursed the boy in half a dozen vulgar permutations equating to the same core principal: a coward. Bernie's long strides carried him closer, but would he be fast enough?

Dexter made a single look back, and what lurked in those eyes was no longer wholly human. Something primal had risen up

64

in them, a being of purest id, and that beast in a man's clothes hungered for escape. With a near snarl, he renewed his attempts to reach the doorway. He no longer tried to clear a path. Instead, he led with his soles, moving up and over the bottleneck, driving people under his boots like so much wheat.

Get him, Bernie . . . Please . . .

But no. Dexter made it out the door before Bernie reached the halfway point of the bottleneck.

Chuck cursed silently. No longer merely at the boy, now he railed against luck or fate or merely the cosmic circumstance that posed as divine whim.

The one hopeful spot in Dexter's frantic escape? If they no longer care for human life, the boy's pursuers could easily follow the trail of broken young that Dexter had made through the pack. Bernie did just that, and Chuck felt a sting in his chest and head with every angry step his friend made. The carpet screamed or wailed, like the lost souls of Hell itself—what tier was it, the home of the damned who remained encased in grey soil but for their faces and heads? What sin were those poor fools guilty of committing whilst still of the flesh? Were they covetous? Lecherous? *Bea would know*, Chuck thought in a wild instant; he reached the door only seconds after the target.

Chuck could not follow. He stopped at beginning of the trail of the battered and turned to look back from whence they had come.

Bodies lay shivering behind him, eyes averted as though he were some avenging angel, no some *Devil*. Around him lay the battered and the bruised. On the rink, one skater had apparently fallen on another and bones had snapped. Along the floor, a blonde girl cried through a facial mask of blood, trying to wipe at her ruined eye, while her equally blonde friend continued to pull her hands away. Closer to the door, a shapely brunette tried to collect the small white lumps of her broken teeth, after either Dexter or Bernie—or, most awful possibility of all, both—had stepped on her mouth. Beside her, a dark haired man with a bloodless face struggled to bend two fingers back in the proper direction.

This place had become Hell, and Chuck felt the weighty responsibility for its construction in his chest. *If Bea were here*, he thought, *she would pray*. He, however, could find no words to offer any form of appeasement.

"I'm— I'm sorry," he said, and it sounded utterly ludicrous coming from his lips, his mouth. Well beyond trite.

He maneuvered through the remains of the bottleneck, trying not to damage anyone further. He experienced only modest success at this endeavor, but did not pause long at his missteps.

The air outside, possibly a touch cooler with evening's arrival, still hugged him, cloying and hot. He looked left then right, saw the chase leading down past the tiny restaurants and hole in the wall record shops, along the lines of parked automobiles, equally shiny whether new or old.

Hot as it was, humidity clutching his throat like death's own hand, Chuck ran after his friend. Three pairs of feet pounded the concrete of long, unfamiliar streets—through the smells of beef and beans, past laundry and florist, hung a right on Ventura and then across and on—until the sun was gone and only the lingering radiance of dusk filled the sky with fading watercolors.

Bernie refused to yield, and therefore Chuck refused.

Within a dozen blocks, after several failed efforts to cut through alleys or dark places in valiant but vain efforts to lose his pursuers, Dexter finally collapsed onto the sidewalk, palms planted on the concrete before him like a man readying himself to do push-ups. The boy gasped for air with his whole body. Sweat poured off him like rain.

Breathing fast but nowhere near as exhausted, Bernie arrived beside the boy. His swagger remained full of rage. He grabbed the back of Dexter's denim jacket, pulled him up and aside, into the brick wall of a tapas restaurant. Inside, a flustered man in a cheap server's uniform squeaked Spanish protests that Bernie ignored.

Chuck arrived to Dexter's shouting for someone, anyone to "Call him off me! Get him off me!"

Chuck said, "Bernie."

No good, no response. The big fellow from the Northeast rammed Dexter's face once more into the bricks.

"Come *on*, man!" Dexter's wails grew blurred and blubbery. "Stop him a'fore he *kills* me—"

Bernie slammed the boy yet again, and this time something snapped in Dexter's face and blood sprayed on the wall.

Chuck grabbed Bernie's shoulder, pulled. Bernie glared back, their eyes locked, and Chuck said, "Ease down, soldier." Calming, calming. Would it work?

After only four seconds of silent contest, whatever had snapped got repaired. Bernie deposited Dexter on the sidewalk, and took a step back, breathing heavy and fuming, but no longer out of control.

The blood, Chuck saw, came from the boy's nose, fat and broken. In the boy's eyes, that animal instinct was gone, replaced now by the pouting misery of a kicked puppy.

Poor baby.

"You hurt a lot of people back there, punk," Bernie said. "Friends of yours."

"I din't do nothing," Dexter said in a stuffed up whine. "It was you and trigger finger Joe, there done the hurting. I was only trying to get out."

"You keep lying," Bernie said, "if it helps you sleep at night."

"We should get off the street," Chuck said. He gestured to an alleyway, and discovered he still had the pistol in hand. He tucked this into his jacket pocket as Bernie "led" Dexter away. Before he joined them, Chuck put ten bucks on the tapas restaurant counter. "For the inconvenience," he said. The fellow acted like he didn't understand English; maybe he really didn't. Chuck could not find the strength to care one way or the other.

In the alley, near a Dumpster that stank of stagnant urine despite its being empty, Bernie released his grip on Dexter's shoulder, and the boy sank once more into a wheezing, exhausted heap.

"I din't do nothing," Dexter said. "I don't know nothing."

"Then why," Chuck asked, "did you run?"

Dexter clapped his trap and stared at the concrete between his legs.

"My friend asked you a question," Bernie said.

"I'm sorry I called you a panty sniffer. And stuff. Okay?" Now, Dexter looked up, eyes wide with hope that the apology, like truth, might set him free. Chuck watched this hope crushed and felt no small amount of satisfaction. "What do you two want from me?"

"I want to know," Chuck said, "How long you've been watching Kingdom Avenue."

"Huh?"

"That's where you met me this morning. Kingdom Avenue. You said you were watching it. How long?"

"I— I don't know. Are you going to kill me?"

Bernie answered this: "Are you going to give us a reason?"

Dexter licked his lips and eyed the long, black tunnel to freedom behind them. "Uh-uh."

"No trouble?" Bernie asked.

"I won't do shit to piss you off."

"Good," Chuck said. "Do you know Selma Kowalski?"

"W-Who? No, man. Who's th-that?"

Bernie and Chuck exchanged brief glances, and then returned the combined might of their glares back to Dexter.

"When was the last time you saw her?" Chuck asked.

"I said I don't know who—"

"Keep lying," Bernie said, "and see how well that does for you."

"I'm—" Perhaps the rest of that sentence was going to be *not lying*, but if so, it remained unspoken after Dexter saw the anger entrenched in Bernie's face. "I don't know. It was like a week?"

"Why are you asking us?" Bernie said. "Don't you know days from weeks from months? Are you too stoned to tell the difference?"

"I'm usually stoned, man." Dexter tried to laugh, but the lonely, slow cheer only made him sound even more isolated. "I—"

"You know Allen Lang?" Chuck asked.

"I— N-no."

Bernie asked, "Where can we find him?"

"Look, man. It ain't as easy as all that."

"So you say." Chuck shifted his weight and leaned down low enough that Dexter could hear his whisper. "Don't give me any shit about how you can't tell us because they'll hurt you. Kill you. We don't care. If you keep running us in circles, here, there's going to be whole vistas of pain that you've never seen in your wildest nightmares. We've seen war, boy. Like your brother. And we've killed before, and the first time is the hardest. I've killed several dozen men since returning from that Hell, and I can assure you I sleep through nights. So why don't you cut the horseshit and tell us what we want to know. When we're satisfied, you're free to go." With a little more volume he asked, "Right, Bernie?"

"You bet."

"How can I trust you?" Dexter asked.

"I don't want your trust," Chuck said. "If you think about it, you've got no real choice."

Dexter licked his lips, again, and Chuck knew the boy was broken.

He felt no pride at this success, merely eager for the answers to come.

#

1968

"Chuck? Is that you?"

It had been over ten years since he'd seen Lucy last, but her voice was still the same. It filled him with an awkwardness, when he turned in the grocery store and saw her down the aisle, standing behind a cart, belly large with child and holding a four year old's hand.

Her face was lined with age and stress, strains of motherhood and the simple act of living. On the ring finger of her left hand, a tarnished band of matrimony.

"Lucy." He felt odd at saying her name. The word, at least in his mind, carried emotions he could no longer access. It was as though his brain had encased that name in a lead box, never to be opened again, and here he was trying to utilize it without breaking the seals. He tried to recover by adding a little too much cheer to the follow up "Hello."

She cocked her head to the side. "Haven't seen you in—"

"Been a while, huh?"

"Yes, Chuck." She raised a hand to her hair, unconsciously smoothing an invisible rough spot. "So. How. How are you?"

"I see you've got a girl?"

"And another on the way," she said, hand now moving to her stomach. "Erig's wanting three, but I feel a little too old for that."

"Erig's the little mister?"

"My darling, yes."

"How long have you . . .?"

"Six years this February."

"Congratulations."

"Ah. Thanks."

Chuck glanced at the girl. "Hello there," he said, "What's your name?"

The child, who had a shock of brilliant white blonde hair and her mother's dazzling blue eyes, merely wiped her nose and tugged a couple of times on her mother's hand. Lucy crouched down, and the girl whispered something in her ear. Lucy listened, and then said, "Nope. Afraid you've got to tell him yourself."

"Margi," the little girl said, "and you're a scary man."

Chuck could not help but laugh. "Sometimes I am."

"Has something happened? Your face . . ."

He touched the white bandage on his cheek, as though having forgotten it. "A little run in with a caustic substance." To Margie, he added, "Whenever you hear Safety Instructions, Margie, from your Mom or Dad or someone in authority, you listen, okay?"

She wiped her nose again. Was it one wipe for yes, two wipes for no?

"You've changed, Chuck. Not quite so averse to little ones?"

"No, not quite the way I was . . ."

"Are you—"

"I don't have— I mean, I'm a godfather. Maybe you remember me talking about Dwight Kowalski? From the army?"

It was plain on her face that she had no such recollection, but she nodded anyway.

"Well, he . . . He contracted some kind of tumors. He passed on, oh, nine years ago?"

"I'm sorry to hear that."

"When he was on his death bed, he asked me to look after . . . Uh. Take care of his little girl. So, I've been a kind of father from afar for her."

She cocked her head as she listened to him, perhaps seeing him in a different light. "Funny. I never thought you'd ever be content around kids."

"A man can be a fool, can't he?"

Her voice became as flat as a penny left on the train tracks. "Yes, he can be."

Emotion swelled in his chest, filling him like a balloon. Words failed, and yet he had so much he wanted to say, he just did not know how to start. Beginnings and middles and ends and where could he find the words to communicate what he was feeling? And would he if he knew how to?

No. She was happy enough, now. No need to open old wounds. He thought about making some excuse and walking on his way, putting the hand cart of groceries back and getting out of the store as quickly as possible, but even those words failed. The will was not there, and without that he was powerless.

"So, are you still living in Brooklyn?"

"Yes," he said, powerless to resist her questions. "Different apartment, though. I travel quite a bit."

"Must be nice to get away."

"It's. It's a life."

"Mommy?" Margie said, tugging on the hand. "I need to pee pee."

Lucy offered him a smile, and he could not tell if it was legitimate or not. "Well, I suppose I'll see you around?"

"I suppose."

She started to walk on, but even after she had gone down the aisle toward the bathrooms, Chuck found he could not actually move. He stood there, for long seconds after she had gone, rooted and broken, wondering about how his life might have been different if he had not walked out on that woman some eleven years before . . .

He did not cry, but he pondered. That was painful enough.

#

1977

The Pinewood Derbyshire was an upscale eyesore, a crescent shaped building with plenty of windows and visible steel beams and apparently half completed walls. Upon seeing it, Chuck had to admit that it served as both a prime example of excessive amounts of wasted money and half-baked ideological architectural theories in equal measures. Where but in California would you find a place like this, which was dedicated not as a museum to the contemporary but to loud music, overpriced drinks, and young folks wandering around a walnut and steel dance floor in choreographed approximations of dancing.

While he had not come here to critique the place, he found himself unable to stop. Perhaps, as the lost boys and girls often claimed, he really was "too old" to appreciate their sense of values. Could that really be the case?

Bernie kept him on course. The two men walked shoulder to shoulder through the room. A completely different crowd than they had just encountered at the rollar rink party place, this group cast occasional concerned eyes toward them—no less bloodshot from chemical exposure than Dexter's bunch—and a kind of half smile, as though the drugs in their systems had stolen their ability to actually carry through with a full show of cheer. The room stank with money, women wore hundred dollar shoes and thousand dollar little black dresses, men wore the equivalent in tuxedos. Chuck and Bernie wore the same mussed up suit coats and slacks they had worn to the Rink, but the amused cattiness never arrived in time to find their faces, only their backs.

At the bar—a slab of two inch thick frosted glass atop blocks of glass bricks illuminated from within by blue and white incandescent bulbs—Chuck slipped a dollar to the bartender. The bill had been folded exactly as Dexter described, and it must have passed muster, since the bartender—a fat man with more hair, and black as a new moon, over his lip than on his sweaty scalp—took it without glancing at it and smiled. While not drug glazed, this smile was no more genuine than any others the men had seen on their way from the front door. Shark grins held more warmth.

The bartender hiked a thumb over his shoulder, indicating a set of glass stairs lined with a steel railing. These led up to a balcony, where the truly wealthy awaited. A slender but dangerous looking bouncer, a bruiser AmerInd mulatto who wore his tux and obvious shoulder holster like second skins, stood at the foot of the stairs and eyed Chuck and Bernie, but then nodded to the bartender. "Top and left," he said. "Table three."

"Your man there let us up?" Chuck asked.

"Who, Chief Zulu?"

What an unfortunate name.

The batender continued, nonplussed. "Pay him no mind. You got the nod, he won't make trouble."

Bernie tapped Chuck's arm and indicated both the stairs and bouncer with a single tilt of his head, and they walked on. The AmerInd mulatto, wearing a permanent frown, watched them as they approached. The bouncer's face showed no more emotion than his eyes, which were as gray as Artic icepack. He studied them as they approached, walked past and then up.

Above waited two dozen tables—inch thick, frosted glass surfaces atop four, welded, wrought iron C-shape supports— surrounded by between two and six matching chairs. At least half the seats were filled with men and women of means, sipping at colorful martinis in stylish glasses or exotic beverages in equally exotic vessels. Though separated by only yards, the tables remained isolated from one another. Few eyes turned toward the stairs as they arrived, but Chuck knew these fellows had certainly taken notice of the new faces.

"Which one is table three?" Bernie said, a subvocal volume for Chuck alone.

Chuck considered the arranged tables and occupants and said, "How about this one?" before approaching his first choice.

Three men and two women sat closely huddled around this table, forgoing their drinks to look up at the new arrivals.

Two of the men were practically twins, certainly related. Nordic featured, with athletic not weightlifter builds, with piercing blue eyes and hair so blonde as to be nearly white. The last man was dark in both hair and complexion, with a narrow scar on his left nostril. The women were both pretty, one was brunette and the other a blonde, and neither was very soft in appearance. These women both wore hardness with the same familiarity as their evening gowns.

Chuck said, "We're looking for Allen."

"Are you?" said the dark haired man.

"Dexter can vouch for us," Bernie said.

One of the Nordic fellows looked toward the dark haired man with that suddenness of surprise, but the dark haired man simply asked "Can he?" with a natural boredom.

You're good, Chuck thought, *but your fellow has given up the game.*

"He can," Chuck said. "And let me cut through the typical crap game. Dexter told us to find you here, told us what you'd look like, told us you were the man to talk to if we wanted to see Allen Lang. Well, we want to see him?"

The blonde woman wet her lips, more than a little nervous. "What do you want to see him about?"

Now, the dark haired man glanced away from Chuck, long enough to cast an irritated glance toward the woman.

"The Rose Devil," Chuck said, and sat down in the last available chair.

Three looks of surprise, one blanche. Only the dark haired man remained inscrutable. "And what makes you think Allen cares about this 'Rose Devil'?"

"Because the son of a bitch killed Allen's mother and has been trying to kill him," Chuck said. "Look, I really don't give two figs about the dope trade. You're Lang's people. You're at odds with The Devil's people. The only thing I give even half of a shit about is Selma Kowalski. You know her?"

The Nordic men's expressions answered that question clearly enough. The dark haired woman asked, "What exactly do you want?"

He met the woman's eyes and found imperfections, flecks the color of flint, in her emerald irises. Those were eyes that had seen horror, perhaps performed by their owner's hands. Chuck felt a chill, but did everything in his power not to reveal it.

These were not human beings he sat amongst. These strangers only wore humanity as a guise over something much darker. He had seen men inured to killing both in Korea and amongst the souldead returnees from that Vietnam debacle. A man who finds pleasure in lifetaking, who then performs this act often enough, murders his own humanity. Oh, he continues to walk among his preferred prey, but he is no longer of them. He is something far beneath his prey. A killer, yes, but performing a death whose only purpose is for pleasure is a sickness. As many as Chuck had killed, he had never once felt pleased with the action. They had all been necessary. These three men and two women waiting at table three were something altogether different.

He recalled old Cave family wisdom, passed from father to son for unknowable numbers of generations, delivered on each son's first journey into the wilds with a rifle.

Theirs was a two sided wisdom. The first part was this: Show no fear, lest the animals smell it and call you prey. The second part was this: One bullet alone delivered with neither glee nor sorrow.

"I want," he said, voice monotone, "my goddaughter. And whomever stands in my way, will wish they had never seen me."

The dark haired woman held his gaze for nearly ten seconds after this, before her eyes broke away. The blonde woman lasted almost fifteen seconds, each twin failed the game of stares after only seven seconds.

The dark haired man, however, did not break at all. After a minute of silent contest, Chuck nodded to him, received a nod in return, and the game was called a draw.

"A couple of tough guys," the chatty twin said. "Is that what you are?"

"Want to try us?" Bernie asked. Chuck glanced his way, and his partner went mute.

"We're not tough," Chuck said, "we're just determined."

The dark haired man brought his hands together in slow, mocking applause. "A fine display, gentlemen. Maybe you want tell us who we're dealing with?"

"We're dealing, Syd?" the quiet-until-now twin asked.

The dark haired man, Syd, licked his lips and raised his eyebrows, as though asking Chuck, *Do you see what I have to work with?* To the speaker, he replied, "You bunch of sorry sacks of shit gave up the game. What would you say we should be doing? Posturing, when we're clearly outmatched?"

Why is he buttering us up? Chuck said nothing, hoped his face was betraying little if anything of the emotional turmoil racking his insides.

"So, Selma's god-daddy," Syd continued, "what should we call you?"

"Chuck."

"So, Selma's god-daddy Chuck, I'm Syd, as you probably already heard. These two Swedes are Ben and Bjorn. She's Emmy," a single nod to the brunette, "and Chloe," a nod to the blonde.

"A pleasure," Chloe said, in a manner that communicated with no obfuscation how little of one, it actually was.

"No Allen Lang," Chuck said.

"We're Allen's," Syd considered the next word carefully, "screen."

"So, how do I meet him?"

Syd's grin was actually a pleasant enough one, it was the kind of good natured, boy next door handsome that could net the heart and loins of any girls he fed it to. "Make me like you."

"You sent three people to Selma's place, yesterday afternoon," Chuck said.

"Perhaps."

"Oh, Max came clean enough."

"This isn't making me like you—"

"The Rose Devil sent two others. I killed them both."

Syd's eyebrows raised a little higher and his eyes took Chuck in anew, reevaluating. "Interesting."

"And I found," Chuck said, "what Selma was holding."

"Did you?"

"Would Allen be interested?"

"In a resourceful fuddy such as yourself? I'm sorry, I mean a resourceful *man*."

"Call it my bargaining chip."

"The holdings for a girl?"

"And a meeting with Lang."

"A bargain at twice the price."

"No need to be an asshole."

"Did you just call me an ass—"

"Asshole," Chuck said. "I called you an asshole. Look, asshole, if I want my peter pumped, I don't need to come to you. I'm not here to impress you, I'm not here to take you out and buy you chocolates and woo your panties off. Just be plain with me."

"'Be plain'?" Syd's humor all but vanished. "How's this? Three responses for you, your buddy, and the both of yous. *Fuck* you, fuck *you*, and *fuck off*. Plain enough?"

"Don't make me shoot you here and now," Chuck said. "I'm in a killing mood, and you aren't helping matters."

"Chuck," Bernie said, and Chuck heard the uncertainty in his partner's voice. Good, if he heard it, so did they. The women glanced their concern at Syd.

"He wouldn't," Syd said, by way of reassuring them of their safety.

"Try me," Chuck said. "I've got Max's gun in my pocket. A full clip of ammunition, one round chambered. An extra pair of clips. One from the towhead, one from the other guy, what did he look like? I can't remember, I killed him too fast. Just like the lot of you. Let's see. First, I'll take the bo-hunks. Then, well, I like blondes better, so I'll save her for last." He counted off as he pointed to each in turn, pointing from one head to another around the table. "One, two," Bjorn then Ben, "three," Emmy the brunette, "Four . . ." Syd, "and Chloe makes five. Two rounds left in the clip." His finger gestured toward one of the other tables. "Maybe for the gunsels you've got planted at other nightspots?"

"He won't kill us," Syd said, confident but for the sweat beading on his temples, "because then he won't find his precious Selma."

"I found you," Chuck said. "You don't believe I can find someone else? No one is so necessary as to be irreplaceable. Not even Allen Lang."

What followed was another stare down between Chuck and Syd. Neither man would relent, would yield their pride, and yet Chuck had put just a sliver of fear into his opponents friends, and as little as Syd might pride himself on being like these sycophants, he was too tightly bound to them to completely resist the emotional assault they offered him.

Don't let him kill us, they communicated silently, and those four voiceless pleas injected just enough weakness that the staring contest lasted one fourth as long as it had before. Syd glanced toward the table, this time, and his exhale communicated absolute weariness.

"I think," he said, "I'm tired of things."

"Syd?" Bjorn asked.

"Let's take him to see Lang."

Chapter Seven

Lang's people rode in a pair of long, black Buicks. Chuck rode in the backseat of one and Bernie in the other, both blindfolded, hands bound behind the back. This was a non-negotiable stipulation. When Chuck raised his ire to protest, Syd replied, "You're getting your wish, but it has to be under our conditions. Kapeesh?"

The Buicks' tires rode across concrete and asphalt, from stop-and-go surface streets to open up and go highway, from honking horn congestion they turned further and further from the city noises. Ellen must've been at the wheel, she was extolling the virtues of cruise control just about every fifteen minutes.

By that gauge, the ride lasted at least ninety minutes before the squeaking brakes pulled the car to a stop, and the engine grumbles ceased in favor of the *plock—plock-plock*s of cooling engine blocks.

"We're here," Syd said. Doors opened.

Chloe's voice, a warm, rose scented breeze carrying an excited whisper, found Chuck's ear, "Slide to the right side, *daddy-oh.*" Even blindfolded, Chuck could see the sneer on her face when she added that *daddy-oh*. All too familiar. Dexter had worn a similar smirk when calling him pops, and these were the latest of a thousand other examples that sprang to mind—most of them from the lips of those at least twenty years his junior. The sneer was youth's ultimate weapon, cool defiance. Chuck knew he had probably talked and acted the same way to his old man, or any random coots he had met when a teen and twentysomething wanderer; that old chestnut that kids respected their elders was rose-colored lenses bullshit.

"Sure thing," he said, trying to sound chipper. Nothing deflated and eradicated cool defiance faster than a cheerful response. The way her breathing changed, the way a low animal sound caught in the back of her throat, made him smile for real.

Some things really did never change. Words could change and so could their associated meanings, but the attitudes did not. Human beings would keep on keeping on right to Armageddon.

Might this insight provide him an advantage?

He considered this as he slid out the car's rear bench seat. Outside, Syd tugged the blindfold off, and light stung Chuck's eyes like a hive of infuriated hornets. Chloe went to work on the handcuffs, and then he was free to rub his wrists and take in the surroundings.

Colorful desert swept away toward the horizon in all directions, while narrow strips of dark concrete, lines of hope and civilized progress, pressed their slender way through the brutal landscape of sand and rock, beginning at one speck of a city beyond the eastern horizon and leading to another near the ocean on the western side of the country.

"Where the deuce are we?" Chuck asked.

Syd's reply came without emotion. "Where you asked to come." He walked across the desert, every step kicking up clouds of grit and dirt. With some urging on the part of Syd's associates, Chuck followed and then Bernie.

Bernie said, "We must be halfway to Vegas, huh?"

Chuck said, "I don't know that we came quite that far."

"Back in the Northeast," said Bernie, "we'd of been driving long enough to see three states."

The others walked with them, staying close enough to make Chuck wary. Syd stopped walking after about one hundred and twenty yards and turned back to face them. "Here we are."

Chuck asked, "But where is here?"

"Where you asked to be." Like that answered anything.

"Enough with the Jim Morrison seek and ye shall find horsehock—"

Syd pointed down to the earth, never once taking his eyes off of Chuck, and said, "Have you no respect for the dead?"

Chuck looked down. A dozen polished, white stones thrust six inches up from the earth like the enormous teeth of some long extinct beast. Someone had taken the care to arrange them in a rough circle approximately eight feet in diameter. Though the wind kicked up dirt, the stones remained unburied, testament to a careful hand and attention.

"What the hell is this?" Bernie asked.

Syd remained mute, so Chuck answered, "This is a grave."

"Indeed," Syd said, "Here lies your enemy, Mr. Chuck. Here lies Allen Lang."

Bernie spat out at least seven syllables in quick succession, various attempts at beginnings, ranging from outrage to outright confusion. Chuck met Syd's eyes and found no lie in them.

"Why did you bury him way the hell out here?" Bernie asked.

"We didn't," Syd replied. "The *real* enemy did. The Rose Devil. If not personally, then he had his soldiers do the deed."

"You dug him up?" Chuck asked.

"Nope," a woman said. Chuck did not glance back to see which one, though it sounded more like the brunette than the blonde. *Emmy.* "The Devil sent us film."

"Film?" Bernie asked, obviously withholding the question, *And you believe it?*

"Allen was a documentarian," Syd said. "He went south, to make a film about drug smuggling. Funds ran dry while he was in Columbia, trapping him in that country. He tried his hand at the business he'd gone to report on and found he had a knack for it. A passion. He took three cameras with him, and returned with only one. That camera was his good luck charm. It was this camera the Rose Devil's men sent back to us. With a loop of film showing Allen digging his own grave. When the hole was deep enough, when Allen was out of sight in that hole, whoever was running the camera put the rig down, walked up to the lip, and shot him. The film ran out before they'd reburied him."

"And you sure this weren't no lie?" Bernie asked.

"No lie," Syd said. "It was the Rose Devil."

"I take it," Chuck said, "he sent you more than the camera and footage."

"He also sent us a map out here."

"Sounds like he was telling you business is over," Bernie said.

"We decided to keep things running," Chloe said. "Allen would've wanted it that way."

"He's still in charge," Ben said, "ask anyone."

"He's in charge in name only, right?" Chuck said. "So you can cut a plea if you're caught? It won't work . . ."

"What do you know?" Bjorn asked.

Chuck almost rose to the baiting. He bit back a retort. Silence fell, but for the wind and the distant sound of a car traveling westbound along that ribbon of highway.

"You met him. Allen is us," Syd said, indicating the circle of five.

"I'm sorry your buddy is dead," Chuck said, "but where's my goddaughter?" He stared intently into the man's face, searching for the signs of falsehood in his next few words. He found none.

"We didn't get a map," Syd said, holding his arms outstretched to either side, palms toward heaven, "but the footage puts her hole out here, too."

Bernie was the one to ask, "*What*?" because Chuck could not move. His muscles were locked, and yet they felt without even the slightest amount of strength.

Syd and his boys responded with unfamiliar words to Bernie, who snapped back like some spitting cobra. Chuck could not understand a one of them. What did their words mean? What did—

Oh Hellfire, he thought, she's dead. Really dead. Oh *no*.

Now his body began to move. Downward, sinking to its knees. He wanted to lunge for Syd, stuff those words back in his gob like licorice. He wanted to pull his own ears off. He did not know what he wanted to do. Something cold and dark closed first around his heart and then his eyes, and it brought with it an awful void. An emptiness, that shook the world until it was a blurry mess, and then there was only the sound of pain springing from Chuck's mouth full formed, and it too made no logical, linguistic sense and yet it communicated everything.

He saw her in his mind, from various years, fragments of her from all ages, mixing one to the next to the next. With each of these visions, Chuck thrust his fists down, onto the earth, feeling the skin strong across his knuckles, feeling the stone crumble at his touch. He saw the child Selma in the graveyard asking about heaven, then he saw the teenager Selma outside his building asking for a home, and then he saw the little girl in her tree railing against needing anyone to protect her, he saw . . . He saw. He saw. Again, he punched the earth, as the streams fell from his eyes and soul, and the cold dark brought shivers to his guts and spine. The humid day vanished, and he shivered as though naked on a glacier in the heart of Artic winter.

Hands found him, then. He raged against them, out of control, swinging like a wild wreck. Training was gone, instincts were clouded, and yet he drove the hands away. Soon, they returned, and came this second time with a soothing sound. Chuck lashed out again, this time the hands did not withdraw. He could not see how or who he struck, the water was too deep. He was drowning in the desert, and he could not claw his way out.

The soothing sound penetrated the water and the moans. Words, again, but this time they made a kind of sense. This time, they . . . "We'll get them, Chuck. Whoever done this. We'll fix their asses." *Bernie.*

"Dear God, I swear," Chuck said, "*I'll kill every one of the fuckers.* I'll . . . With these hands, I'll . . ."

Vision returned, swimming through the murky downpour, and he saw the torn skin of his knuckles, the blood so brilliant under the sun. The fingers he still clenched in fists, tight and shaking, and he wanted something to batter, to ruin with them.

"I'll kill them," Chuck said.

Bernie nodded.

"I swear I will."

"No," Bernie said, his voice a delicate whisper that might shatter if handled poorly, "*We* will."

Friend held friend among the circles of strangers and stones, until the rage eclipsed the sorrow, and there was no more room for tears, only fury.

#

Soon, they rode in the cars, again.

Chloe sat beside Chuck, and her tone took on a sympathic tone. Chuck could not tell if it was real. "You really love her, daddy-oh." No more snideness, this time. More of a shock. Amazement at the depths of Chuck's affections—as though she could tease the depths out of him.

"She is the most important . . ." He fell silent, leaving the thoughts unspoken.

"Were you serious?" Syd asked. "About wanting to avenge her?"

Chuck did not deem that worthy of a response.

"Because there is a way," Syd said, pausing with a poor actor's dramatic timing.

"I'm listening."

"The Rose Devil has a man in our own little group," Syd said. "Riding in the second car. With your friend. An agent."

Chloe could not stay quiet at this news. "There's a traitor? Is it Ben? Bjorn?" Who?"

"Hush," Syd said, "our friend here will find him out."

"How long have you known about this?" Emmy asked, her knuckles white on the steering wheel.

"For three months."

"Syd, you—" Chloe slapped him, and he took it without complaint. She was not satisfied. That first blow was tantamount to the dam breaking, and what followed was a flood of flailing; mostly these struck the passenger's seat headrest, a few found their way past. Her voice became a frantic shriek of vulgarity and accusation.

Syd accepted less than twenty seconds worth, before he punched her in the face. The blow, a jab to her mouth, brought her back to her senses. Her lower lip had split on her teeth, and she sat with her hands in her lap, catching the blood.

"You," she said, "You could've saved Allen. Or Selma. Or . . . *Robbie*."

"I couldn't," Syd said, "without giving up the game. Allen knew. He . . . told me not to let on." To Chuck, Syd added, "He told me about something you probably have a greater grasp on. In the Big One, Dubya-Dubya-Eye-Eye, the Allies had some kind of codebreaker that cracked the Germans communications. Right around the time of D-Day, and they found out about some big German move that'd cause a lot of problems for innocent folks. Well, they had a choice as to whether or not to reveal they'd cracked the code by intercepting the Germans in time to save folks or let innocent people suffer so that D-Day would go without a hitch. What do you think they chose to do, huh, 'daddy-oh'?"

"You shouldn't hit women," Chuck said. The pout revealed this was not the response Syd was hoping for.

"Syd," Emmy said, "stop being so—"

"Shut it, Emmers," Syd said. "We knew what we were doing."

"You were playing with peoples' lives," Chloe said.

"No," Chuck said, "he's doing that now."

"What do you mean?" Emmy asked.

"I mean *he's* the traitor," Chuck said, "He's the snitch, the 'narc'. Syd here knows the Rose Devil, and he's been reporting back to his real master, and now he's trying to get me to kill off each of you."

Syd stared at Chuck with a slack jaw. Three voices spoke in unison, and it was nearly impossible to identify who said what: "I— How—- *What*?"

Then, the women went nuts, and Syd started digging into his inside jacket pocket, but Chuck pulled his pistol first. Too bad Chloe shoved past him, knocking the gun aside and off target. Chuck's bullet did not catch Syd solidly in the shoulder, but instead went through the meat of his right arm. The bullet punched through the windshield, spattering the surrounding fractures with some blood. Not enough to prevent Syd's retrieving his own weapon. The gun came free, but then Chloe was upon him, slapping and punching and clawing. Her nails caught his face and dug ragged grooves through the flesh. Chuck tried to pull her back, to get her clear of the man's weapon and to give himself a clear shot at the man.

Syd started to bring his pistol to bear on Chloe. She saw this, grabbed his wrist and jerked it away. Chuck shouted, "*No*," as the gun went off and caught Emmy in the ear. She rocked in the driver's seat, and a chunky mess sprayed out the side of her head, coating the window and door and covered Chuck's face like a warm mask. The car veered wildly off the road, into the desert. The engine still growled, and Chuck recalled her fascination with cruise control.

They were blazing into the desert at a steady sixty-five miles per hour, in an out of control car.

Chloe and Syd were still at odds, the man trying to shoot her while she gave him all hell's fury, and Chuck had to make the split second decision: car or combat?

Tires jounced across the earth, and the car rolled dangerously from side-to-side. If we flip, we're fucked, Chuck thought. He tried to go over the driver's side headrest. His shoulders, head and arms made it, but the chest got caught up between that off white vinyl encased, molded plastic and the velour roof above. He stretched past the corpse, and found his fingers could not quite reach the wheel.

Syd's gun fired a second time, and this round whinged past Chuck's back, poppin through the roof. Chuck brought his gun around and held steady for a moment, then squeezed off. The bullet ripped through Syd's wrist. Syd's gun dropped in the passenger side footwell and the brilliant sprizer of blood sprayed Chloe in the eyes. She screamed louder curses, but did not let go of him, started shaking him as though he might come to pieces if she did a good enough job.

The steering wheel was a solid rectangular centerpiece several inches wide, and about a foot long, which connected to the steering column, but the actual wheel had several inches of clearance at the top and bottom. Chuck jabbed his gun like a pointer into this clearance, and banged it down onto the centerpiece. He could make some basic, extremely coarse directional alterations this way, but the wheel required something a lot steadier. Two hands say . . .

The wheels hit a large rock with the sound of a small explosion, and the car jerked sideways. The corpse bounced in its seat, clubbing Chuck with one of its limbs in a nearly comical flail.

A new plan formed.

He tossed his gun into the back seat and grabbed the dead woman's shoulders. Moved further down. Grabbed her elbows, yanked them forward, jamming the corpse's hands through the steering wheel. Synchronizing movements of the arms up and down, the wrists would apply a steady pressure to the centerpiece. He could control the damn car.

Syd shoved Chloe off of him, and reached down into the passenger footwell. Going for his gun.

Oh no you don't. Chuck played Emmy's arms up and down like a frantic drummer, and the car veered side to side, jouncing up and down on some of the worst terrain.

Syd's head cracked against the panel, and he clutched at it with his off hand. This only resulted in more pain, and then Chloe was back on him, and scratching, going for his eyes.

Our only hope, Chuck thought, *is to get this thing out of cruise control.* He had never driven a car with that feature, and so could not say what switch controlled it or where said switch might be located. *Have to hit the brakes*, he thought. *But how?*

Chuck brought the car back around, aiming toward the road. More rough terrain, made Emmy's lifeless body bob and bounce in the seat. With a little jimmying, could he get her foot to hit the brake? Maybe. Or maybe—

Syd's door sprang open, and the man went out into the desert with a scream. The door started swinging back, but bounced open once more. The stupid sack was hanging on to the door jam. His eyes were wide and white, his mouth open and screaming and catching plenty of the dirt cloud that the car had kicked up and was now returning through.

"Girl," Chuck said, "Chloe."

"Oh my God, oh my God, oh my God."

Had she not noticed the dire situation? "Get up here. I need you to crawl down and hit the brake."

"Emmy's dead, man. Emmy's *dead*."

"I need you to get up here and—"

"Jesus, daddy-oh, we're fucked!"

"*Shut up*. Get up here and get the fucking break. *Now*."

She slid between the seats, pausing to stare at the ruins of Emmy before she said, "I won't be able to get my feet down there."

"Crawl down there if you have to, damn it."

Like an eel, she slid. A serpent across the bench seat's leather upholstery and down into the footwell. "I *can't* . . . I *found it*—"

With a sharp shriek, Syd snatched her calf and yanked her across the seat, away from the brake and toward the open door. Even though he was using his blasted hand, he still had the strength of terror on his side.

Chuck stabbed the corpse's arms into the wheel and played them like drumsticks, putting the car into a hard one hundred eight degree turn, and Syd had to release Chloe to keep hold of the doorframe. Chloe slid back across the seat, out of the man's reach and back down into the footwell. She used both hands on the brake pedal, and the car's brakes screamed, as the chassis jolted and jounced and threatened to come apart, but slowed, slowed, stopped.

Syd's hold, precarious at best, was not enough to fight momentum and keep him on the decelerating vehicle. He bounded forward, cracking against the open door, and then bounced across the earth like a runaway basketball.

Soon enough, the car was still, and the only sounds inside was the soft noise of Chloe weeping. Chuck was up in an instant, locating his own gun, and out the car, moving for the discarded man.

Syd was a tough son of a bitch, Chuck had to admit. He was trying to crawl away despite his blasted wrist. The man's legs followed after him like kite tails.

"Where you going, Syd?"

The man rolled onto his back, then, though his legs mostly remained face down. His face was a mess of blood and grit, his nose was gone, leaving a terrifying gaping hole in the man's puss.

He whimpered for a while, and soon enough Chuck realized he was repeating, "Shoot me."

"Not yet," Chuck said. "I want some answers."

Then, two other guns fired, and the ground spat up chunks about a yard away. There was no real cover, so Chuck dove flat on the ground. Who?

"*You're a dead man,*" one of the twins shouted.

"*You and your buddy, too.*"

Syd started to cough and gurgle an approximation of laughter.

The damned twins didn't know the score. They had been in the other car, out of the loop of conversation and only seeing something crazy going on in the car ahead. Of course they would assume Chuck was the source of the problem. Their method for dealing with that problem was simple enough: first kill Bernie, then Chuck. This flowed through his mind in an instant, spurred on by curses at his own stupidity.

Hopefully Chuck would not have to kill these men. A glance showed them standing side-by-side on the opposite side of the car, one aiming his weapon in Chuck's direction, while the other was keeping his pistol trained on the second Buick's back seat, presumably on Bernie. At least that suggested Bernie was still alive. Shit, he thought, maybe I am going to have to kill these guys.

"Shoot him," Syd howled, and the twin pointing his gun—was it Ben? Chuck could not say for certain, not that it actually mattered terribly much—tried to do just that. Range and lousy nerves worked against him: the gun shook too damn much to be accurate.

"You fellows have to get this straight," Chuck said. "Syd's—"

"Throw down your gun," one said, "and maybe we'll listen."

In that instant, Chuck realized they were beyond listening. It had been a long car ride since he shamed them, threatened them on the second floor of the Derbyshire. Left that long to stew in

87

their own juices, to bicker between themselves, they would be hungry for blood. No matter how he acted at the grave, what he swore, they would still want him dead. Whether they got their wish before or after he took out their opposition was ultimately immaterial.

Hellfire, he thought. He scrambled toward Syd and shoved his gun under the wounded man's jaw. Manic with the pain, quite probably insane, he did not stop laughing, merely continued to stare through Chuck, through the empty blue sky and cackle like a lunatic. I don't need him to notice me.

"Drop the guns, cut Bernie loose and then we'll talk about Syd, here."

The twins appeared to be discussing this. Shit, shit, shit. Using the fellow who had been an equally big pain in their ass to bargain for Bernie's life probably was not the wisest thing to do. Still, if they were discussing, then only time would tell.

The twin with his gun trained on the backseat of the car fired, and Chuck heard Bernie's start hollering. Threats through his obvious agony.

"Ooops," the twin aiming his gun at Chuck said. " Still it's only a flesh wound. Your choice is simple: kill Syd, and we'll kill your pal before we kill you. Toss the gun and you might walk out of this."

Might, but probably not.

A new voice rang out, now. "What the hell are you two doing?" Chloe, blood spattered and emerging from the car. The twins did not expect this.

Really, Chuck thought, *who would*? Come on, Chloe, talk your friends down . . . Don't make me kill them.

"Chloe? What the hell happened to you?"

"Syd's the traitor. Syd was trying to have us killed."

Wrong way to start the negotiations. Especially since the twins now both glared at Syd and Chuck, seeing them together and somehow associating them, as though Chloe herself might have somehow defeated both men and caused them to be lying on the ground together.

Chuck felt the thin flame of hope flicker, as in a strong breeze. Bernie, not the twins, was the one to actually snuff it.

Bernie did not know what was going on. If he had known, he probably would not have tried to jump the twin what shot him. Maybe then, there would have been far less bloodshed.

Then again, if wishes were dollars, then beggars would fly on the Concorde.

Chapter Eight

The sun had fallen far along its downslope but was still at least two hours from evening. For the moment, it hung like the wide eye of some ancient, jaundiced and judgmental god, basking everything in the glaring haze of its sweltering gaze. The landscape was, for the most part barren along here. A ditch ran through the earth toward Chloe's car, and a few scrubby looking, thick-fleshed plants sprang from the cracks, broad leaves held like the hands of hostages.

Syd, blurry-faced and wide-eyed, coughed up blood, and that brought momentary cessation to his giggling. "They're going to kill us," Syd said. And then, just loud enough that everyone might hear, he added "*Partner*."

That's it, Chuck thought.

Then, Bernie lunged from the Buick's backseat, grabbed the twin who had shot him, and they started to dance the frantic steps of two men trying to gain the upper hand. Twin number two turned to see what was going on, and Chuck made his decision. He was on his feet in a flash, bolting for the car, charging like some cavalryman, gun pointed like a saber.

Chloe howled for everyone to stop, to chill, to throw down the guns and give peace a chance. No one listened.

The free twin—Chuck saw it actually *was* Ben—brought his gun to bear on Bernie, hoping to blast the veteran to Hell, to finalize the job his brother had begun with a flesh wound.

Chuck squeezed his trigger, and the gun leapt in his hand. Running and firing, his aim was for crap. Still, that cartridge smacked the side panel of the car with an audible *ping*.

Ben jolted, pulled his head down as though he might spontaneously develop a turtle's shell or other protection if he only got his head low enough, and spun around, once again returning to face Chuck's direction.

Bernie had let one of Bjorn's hands loose—not the gun hand—in order to clobber him twice in the side. One of those was a solid blow to the kidneys, and Bjorn curled, his face a mask of pain.

Chuck fired again, and this time the cartridge caught the hood of the car, ricocheted off apparently near Ben, who finally dropped out of sight. *Hellfire.*

Another shot rang out—Ben firing from cover—and Bernie went down, lying in facedown, a panting heap in the dust and wind. Bjorn brought his own gun up toward the back of Bernie's head about the time that Chuck reached the car.

He put a round into Bjorn—a hip wound—before he slid across the hood and came down almost right on top of Ben, spoiling that man's follow-up blast. Chuck's foot caught the gun hand, and the force of the drop dragged it to the ground, pinning the man long enough for Chuck to tap the warm barrel of his .45 against the man's crown and say, "Howdy, Benny."

Behind him, Bjorn tried to bite back the pain of being shot, but the emotion colored every word that fell out his mouth: "You leave my brother be, you son of a bitch."

"I think we need to take a breath, here," Chuck said. "You need to toss the piece, or I'll splatter Benny's brains on the tire."

"You won't let us go," Bjorn said.

"How long do you want your brother to live? Huh?"

"Bjorn," Ben said, "drop the gun."

Bjorn's shock outweighed his agony. "*What*?"

"He said 'drop the gun', Bjorn."

"Fuck you, man." The words came without energy, merely a response made because it seemed somehow necessary. Still, the man's gun hit the road with a telltale *clunk*.

"Good job, Bjorn. Now it's your turn, Benny."

Ben released the pistol, and as Chuck stepped off of him, he kicked the weapon away.

"Go join your brother, Benny."

The Nordic twins reunited, and Chuck moved to his friends' side. "Bernie. You still alive?"

No answer. *Hellfire.*

Chuck stopped staring at the twins long enough to see the man's body shift with a breath. Shallow, barely there, but he was still alive. Chuck rolled his friend over, saw the wound and gasped.

Bernie's left eye was a mess. The cartridge must have caught him at an angle, it had blasted through the man's nose, and then up into his eye, then out through the brow.

"Oh Jesus, Bernie," Chuck whispered. "Oh Jesus."

The other wound, what Ben had called the flesh wound, was in the meat of Bernie's right side. Chuck felt his breath catch in his throat. "You stupid sons of whores," he whispered. "We were on your side."

The twins said nothing. Their gazes were equally cold and from across the glacier.

The crack of a pistol split the ensuing stillness, this came from behind. The twin looked back the way Chuck had come, toward Syd, and Chuck felt a burst of cold fire turn his insides to glass. He turned back to see, and all movements felt irrationally slow. He knew what to expect, but it still came as something of a surprise.

Chloe stood over Syd, as still as a statue, her right arm curled around her chest, fist poised at her throat holding something—a necklace perhaps—while her left hand aimed Syd's pistol down at him. The slide was back, the weapon was empty, and a thin trail of smoke slithered out the barrel, curling and vanishing in the air.

Syd himself lay before her, body shaking like jelly in a bumped bowl. A red mess like some particularly chunky cranberry sauce surrounded his head in the dust.

Fuck, he thought. *How will I trace the trail back to the Devil, now?* More importantly: *How will I find her grave?*

"So, will you kill us now, too?" Ben asked.

Glancing back, Chuck discovered neither of the brothers had even attempted to move. There was no rage, just a strange isolation, as though reality itself had suddenly cast him out. His mouth was dry, his throat closed. Words were impossible.

"Yes, he is," Bjorn said. "He wants to kill the whole world."

Why would I kill you? Chuck wanted to ask. *I'm not in the same league of scum that your buddy out there is. Was. I'm . . .*

Hellfire, she's certainly lost, now. Selma was somewhere under the desert. Only the Devil knew where, and he wasn't talking. Oh, but he *would* if Chuck ever caught up with him. *When* Chuck caught up . . .

A crunching approached. Chloe's shoes on the rocky grit. "He killed Emmy," she said.

"And now he's going to kill us," Ben said, trying to stab Chuck with dirty looks.

"No. *Syd* killed Emmy," she said through new found tears. "He was working for the Devil. He killed Allen and Selma. He killed *Robbie*."

Whoever this Robbie had been, his name carried more weight than either of the others. Ben and Bjorn looked from her to Chuck, ashamed and uncertain. "What now?" Bjorn asked.

Still, he could not speak. Language had abandoned him. Chloe spoke for him, and her words made sense. "Now, you get up, help that fellow into the car, and we get back to LA. We aren't friends, but nobody's going to kill anybody else. Okay?"

Ben and Bjorn glanced at one another, then returned Chuck's cool gaze. "Works for us."

Finally, enough language returned for Chuck to say to Chloe, in a halting approximation of English, "I really wish . . . you hadn't . . . killed him."

"I'm not sorry I did it," Chloe said, her right hand still clutched something around her throat, a necklace. "He killed my . . ."

"This Robbie . . . was close to you?"

"Robbie was her fella," Ben said.

Chuck found he could not blame her. He was too hollow for such an emotion as blame. He was disconnected. Chuck said, "I would've done the same, eventually. But, after he told me . . ." No, his mind warned, don't go there. Once you start down that path, there was only madness awaiting a man. "Can you keep these two in line?"

Chloe nodded. "Nobody's going to be trouble, now."

"Do you people have anyone you go to," Chuck asked, "for this sort of thing?"

"This sort of thing?" Chloe asked.

"Gunshots," Chuck said. "Did Allen use a trusted doctor? Somebody who knows how not to ask questions?"

Ben said, "We got someone, yeah."

"We do?" Chloe asked.

Ben said, "You never wanted to get involved with that part of what we—"

"That's where we're going," Chuck said, "when I get back."

"Back?" Chloe asked.

Chuck did not reply. Instead, he stumbled away, into the desert, back to the side of the fallen corpse. He was no stranger to gunshot wounds, so the grisly remnants did not startle him with the raw power or shock of just how much damage a .45 slug could do to a human throat at close range. Still, he stared at the man with something akin to regret—*such a waste*—before he knelt and slowly examined the contents of the man's pockets. He hoped for a clue, for a lead, for somewhere to go next.

He found a matchbook from a Chinese restaurant, a ring of keys, a wallet, and a spare magazine for a nine-millimeter pistol. "Even dead," Chuck whispered, "you're damn useless . . . Rest in hell."

Chuck trudged back to the Buick, and the long car ride back to LA.

They rode in silence for nearly twenty minutes: the twins sat up front, keeping their hands where everyone could see them. Chuck and Chloe filled the back bench seat on either side of the still unconscious Bernie. Chloe held a makeshift bandage over Bernie's ruined eye. Then, Ben said, "I never thought you'd turn, Chloe?"

"I'm not turning on anyone."

"Like shit," Ben said, his voice nearly cold enough to frost the inside of the windshield. "You're siding with that . . . That *maniac*."

"He's no maniac. He saved my life."

"He killed Emmy."

"No," Chloe said. "Syd did. We were wrestling over the gun, and Syd fired, and the bullet hit her in . . ." Her words fell to near silence, as realization came over her. "Oh Jesus. *I* killed her. I. Jesus . . ."

"Syd killed her," Chuck said.

"Yeah, you keep talking, pops," Ben said, "Whisper in as many ears as you want. I, for one, won't be killing Desdemona just cuz you say it's right."

"What the hell are you talking about?" Chloe asked. "Who the fuck is Desdemona."

"Othello, man," Ben said. "Your buddy there is Iago, talking to cloud people's minds."

"I'm like the Shadow, now?"

"I got your number, pops," Ben said. "I got it, and the scams you run won't work on me."

Chloe stared wonderment at Chuck. "Do you have any idea what this loon's talking?"

Chuck asked, "What were you, Ben?"

Ben's hands tightened on the wheel. "Huh?"

"Before you got into the big time drug biz. What were you before all this?"

"I was . . . I was an actor."

"A wannabe more like it," Bjorn said. Brotherly teasing.

"Stage?"

"Yeah," Ben said, wariness invading his voice. He was looking for all the angles. "But I was trying to break into the silver screen. Ain't that why most folks come to LA?"

"Thought so," Chuck said.

"Why?"

"*Othello*. It was a stage play," Chuck said, "About a warrior prince who is tricked into murdering his own wife because of rumors of infidelity."

"So, how's he stop it?" Chloe asked.

"He doesn't."

"This guys kills his wife? On hearsay?"

Chuck said, "Yep."

"Well, that's a happy ending," Chloe said. "Was this play a success?"

"It has a following," Chuck said.

"I'll never understand that," Chloe said. "Some folks just got no taste."

"I'm not feeling so good," Bjorn said, and that ended the conversation pretty well for the next ten minutes.

After this sizeable quiet, Chuck asked, "How well did any of you really know Syd?"

"So-so," Chloe said. "We worked together, sometimes we partied, but Syd kept to himself a lot. A moody bohemian type."

"Figures," Chuck said. "Anything I can use to trace him back to the Devil?"

"You really think he was working for the Devil?" asked Ben.

"Yes," Chloe said, voice drowning in sarcasm, "*we really think that*."

"I think you might."

"Have you got something to say?" Chuck asked.

"Only that Syd spent a lot of time at Manchurian Smoke," Ben said, "a chink eatery. Not bad but pricy."

Chuck fumbled the matchbook he'd found out of a pocket. On the black glossy cover, gold embossed letters spelled out the words Manchurian Smoke in a half circle around a piggish faced Mongol. On the rear side, in similar gold embossed lettering, the slogan "Hong Kong Fun!" and an address.

So, perhaps Syd was not such a useless sack of shit, after all.

Chloe asked, "Do you think that's a step toward the Devil?"

"I don't know," Chuck said. "But I plan on finding out."

They were in sight of the city limits when Bjorn let out a groan and slumped in the seat, head against the passenger side window, and would not respond to anything anyone was saying. Not to Chuck, not Chloe, not Ben. Bernie, still unconscious, kept his trap clapped, probably for the best.

Chuck, seated immediately behind the unresponsive man, moved up close behind, and reached up to shake the man, and it was then that he caught sight of all that blood. The smell of it had already been strong on them, but that was from the gore in the desert. This, however, being new blood, did not particularly stink of anything.

Bjorn was bleeding out fast. His life fluids were all over the door handle, and wet puddles on the seat and beneath it. "Hellfire," Chuck whispered, "Bjorn's worse than I thought."

This news lit the fire of panic. Ben muttered his brother's name at two-second intervals, interspersing this with pleas or damnations of a most vulgar sort.

"Shut up," Chuck said, "you aren't helping. And keep your blasted attention on the *road*."

Ben would not listen. His only concern was for his brother.

"How far until your medic?" Chuck asked.

No response. Chuck's voice raised, as he repeated the question, and this time, Ben's response came promptly.

"About twenty minutes?"

"Don't you know?"

"Twenty minutes."

Then, Bernie started to come back around, and Chuck said, "Try to make it in ten minutes or less."

Eleven minutes later, they pulled to a stop behind a nondescript cube of a four-story office building—the kind of brown brick façade that often housed a dozen or so company offices and struggling, occasionally legit businessmen—and Ben muttered a quick, "Stay in the car," before running inside, searching for someone, anyone who might be able to help.

Within moments, a tall, gaunt man with dark complexion and a starched, white uniform emerged. He did not walk so much as lever himself from foot to foot. Ben came alongside and then ahead of him, smiling and gabbing frantically about prognoses, behaving like nothing less than an overly excited puppy.

At the car, the stranger leaned down and scratched at the whiskers on his chin. Chuck noted a knobby pair of cysts on his forehead, arranged without symmetry, like the horns of a goat.

"You see, Mutt?" Ben asked, "You see what I was saying?"

The stranger's voice was a gravely growl when he said, "You weren't lying, Ben." Then, he rose, turned back toward the building, brought both the thumb and middle finger of his right hand to his mouth and blew a pair of short, sharp whistles.

At this summons came a pair of gurneys manned by sweaty faced men in similar looking uniforms. Nervous looking devils they were, and wary. Still, they attended the man called Mutt like a Master Sergeant, and followed his brief orders to the letter, unloading the two wounded men, binding them to the gurneys with four inch wide, dun colored straps, and then hustling them back inside.

Chuck stared into the lines of Mutt's face for the few seconds before that man followed his fellows and he read a cold, calculated power there. This was a man used to being master of his own domain. Ben started to follow after, concern for his brother making him obviously

"Is this Mutt a good doctor?" Chloe asked.

"Actually, he's a dentist," Ben said, "who flunked out of medical school."

Chuck felt a sinking in his gut and a resurgence of that cold, that frosty dread.

Inside the rear door, an unloading area and connection to a freight elevator. When the doors on this last opened, Mutt and his men moved inside first, followed closely by the Chuck and the others. Even with the two gurneys, the fit was not terribly much.

Mutt lit a cigarette as the elevator rose, and took a pair of thoughtful puffs. The smoke trailed out either side of his mouth like steam. He eyed Chuck and Chloe warily. Mutt asked, "Where's Syd?"

"Dead," Ben said. "Devil's men shot him in the desert."

Satisfied with this answer, Mutt nodded to this answer sagely. "And who are these two?"

Ben pursed his lips before he said, "They're friends. Of Syd's."

Mutt made no attempt to hide his study and approval of Chloe's figure. "Nice," he said. Then, the elevator made a soft chime, and the doors opened onto the materials receiving area of Mutt's fourth floor practice. The place was typical low end business chic: once white walls colored by one too many cigarettes, a thin gray carpet, and cheap furniture.

Mutt's men unloaded the elevator quickly, wheeling the gurneys through a nearby door marked Private. Mutt followed after, pausing this time to hold the door for Chloe to walk through first. He watched her derrierre and repeated, "Nice," before letting the door fall into Chuck's waiting hand.

"Thanks," Chuck said.

Mutt casually ignored him. Beyond the door was a small clinic setup. Tools and hospital gear, walls that were mostly soundproofed.

"So, we've got gunshot wounds?" Mutt asked. "Is either man allergic to anything I should know about?"

"Bjorn's allergic to strawberries," Ben said.

"There goes that treatment," Mutt said, without a hint of a smile. "How about medication allergies?"

"Sulfa," Ben said. "He's allergic to sulfa. And the other one?"

Ben looked to Chuck. "He's your pally."

"I don't know," Chuck said. "I should, and I think I did once, but . . . I don't anymore."

"Well, then," Mutt said. "I'll ask you all to leave so that I can do my work."

One of Mutt's men waved his arms like brooms, sweeping the trio back out the door, to the room outside. Chloe plopped down onto the room's cheap couch and waited. Ben stood beside the door, listening to the wall. Chuck paced.

"How well do you trust this guy?" Chuck asked. "Has he ever fucked up?"

"He does good work," Ben said. "And he disposes of . . . any fuck ups."

"Is this a regular thing for you people?" asked Chloe.

Chuck asked, "What kind of a track record does this quack have?"

Ben thought about it. "He's good for maybe sixty percent."

"You're kidding."

"Most of the folks we bring in are on death's door."

"Where do you think Bernie is? Or your brother?"

"They're gonna be okay. They're—"

"I hope so, Benny," Chuck said. "Hellfire do I hope so."

Chloe said, "I'm sure it'll turn out okay."

"Your lips," Chuck said, "to God's ears." Suddenly, he felt the world crash around him. Selma was dead and her body hidden away. If Bernie died, too . . . Somewhere, in the back of his mind, Chuck heard laughter and he knew it belonged to the Rose Devil. Chuck buried his face in his hands. The Rose Devil, whoever that was, would not get away with this. Not with doing what he'd done to Selma.

He was responsible for everything lousy. No matter if it killed Chuck to make it happen, that Devil was done.

The couch springs squawked as weight left them, then Chloe was before him, pulling Chuck's hands from his face, and trying to hold his eyes. She did not like what she found lurking in them, that much was obvious. In the way she jolted and in the way her lips parted with surprise. Still, she stayed near enough to offer some kind of support.

"I'm sure he will pull through—"

"I need to go out," Chuck said.

"To that place? To Manchurian Smoke?"

Chuck nodded. "I need to break a few heads, I think."

"Don't let yours get broken, too."

"I'll try not to." He snickered before he said, "Pray for me, huh?"

"My grandmother always said, 'Pray to God, but row for shore.'"

"I always heard that as 'Pray for the best, expect the worst'. But it's sound advice however you put it." Then, Chuck faced Ben and said, "If Bernie dies," pointing a judgmental finger, "then you do, too."

Ben could not hold Chuck's gaze. He said nothing, merely stared at his toes. Chuck pulled away from Chloe, and he felt her gaze as he strode to the elevator, thumbed for the car, entered it and then descended to the first floor. He could still feel her watching him as he strode out the building and away, into the muggy, smoggy LA night.

#

A cab ride later, Chuck stood outside of the eyesore called Manchurian Smoke, still feeling rage boiling in his bowels. The two story building squatted alongside the road like a whore offering a spread legged invitation. Garish neon reds and golds mingled with traditional Chinese architecture to create a stomach churning gluttony of the senses. Even with the front door closed, the area stank of grease, cooking oil, charred meat, and spilled booze. At either side of the building stood tall gray walls, what other aberrations of tasteless exuberance did they hide away from the senses?

Chuck's back rose, and he entered.

A pair of ebony doors with peeling, faux gold trim opened onto a colorful foyer. Much of the color came from massive aquariums on either side of the room, both filled with brilliant blue water, rainbow hued coral and rock formations, as well as multi colored, exotic fish. At the far end, behind a cash register, stood a bored looking Chinese man in his early twenties. The whiskers on his chin were thick and curling, his hair was longish and unkempt, and he was picking at his teeth with a toothpick fished out of the basket marked "complementary".

At Chuck's entry, the fellow glanced his way with no more feeling than a crocodile. Chuck said, "I'm a friend of Syd's."

When the fellow asked, "How do you know that jerk?" in perfectly unaccented English, Chuck felt momentarily stunned. This was quickly replaced with embarrassment—why should he expect a man to be foreign? Didn't Americans come in all shapes and sizes and skins?

"We met through a mutual friend," Chuck said.

"Yeah, that's nice," the kid said in a way that communicated he could not care less if he tried. "I guess you'll be wanting his table, then."

"I guess so."

"Nice and private," the kid said. "You're early. The others aren't here yet."

"Oh? When do you expect them?"

"Didn't Syd say?"

Chuck's lips met and turned down in a frown. "Maybe I forgot."

"Well, then maybe you'll be surprised," the Chinese kid fished a menu out of the roster behind the counter. "Follow me, pops." Then, he led Chuck on a whirlwind tour of the restaurant.

Most of the customers were dining in the rather expansive main section. Though every table had a light overhead, the ceiling was two stories up and decidedly unfinished looking, leaving plenty of unlit corners for shadows. No families dined here, only couples or groups of well-dressed men, several of whom glared in Chuck's direction when the Chinese kid led him through. He walked past without a word, feeling the glares digging into his back like daggers.

The kid finally led him to a set of sliding, chestnut doors set in the back. Each was adorned with the same red symbol, a hash mark combination of lines and dashes in the general shape of an ancient Chinese temple.

"Does that mean anything?" Chuck asked, indicating the door symbols.

"It means Armored House," the kid said, pulling open the doors and revealing a well-lit, private banquet hall. Polished wooden beams the color of smoke rose along the cream colored walls. The ceiling itself was of a similar smoke color, and gleaming in the glow of the four large windows overlooking a lush garden—filled with greens and golds, reds and oranges, exotic plants one and all—alongside the building. The gray walls Chuck has seen out front of the place surrounded this growing place, hiding the beauty from the passing world. In the center of the room stood a pair of tables and enough settings and high backed chairs for twenty people. Sedate and classy, this room was the eye of the tacky and sensory overloading tornado of the rest of the establishment. As soon as Chuck entered, the boy closed the doors, to keep prying eyes away from this sanctum.

The boy asked, "You interested in an aperitif?"

"No, I'm fine." Chuck considered the two tables. "Lot of people, huh?"

"Not this many. Only about a dozen or so, but you like your privacy."

"Is there a decorum I should respect?"

"Well, I've only ever seen them sit along that far table," the boy said, "without putting their back to the doors. Don't worry, I'm certain they'll be here shortly to fill in the blanks."

"You got a name?"

The boy smiled, and the expression was an impish one. "Chin. And please do me the honor of not adding a 'k'."

"You got it, Chin."

The boy paused at the doors, hands on the ornate, brass handles. "I don't believe you're supposed to be here." Suddenly, Chuck felt his blood turn to icewater. "They never ask me my name. They never make friendly. They have a purpose, and they execute it without causing much of a ruckus or leaving an impression."

"Well, I don't intend to cause a ruckus, either," Chuck said.

"That's a bummer," the boy certainly sounded disappointed. "I had hoped you might shame them into common courtesy."

"We'll see," Chuck said. "Though I have no intention of starting anything, they might not be so restrained."

"Indeed," Chin said, the word colored with wistful hope. "I shall speak no word of your presence here. Let them be surprised."

Chin opened and closed the doors with barely a sound, and soon Chuck was alone in the room. He glanced out the window at the garden, and then considered the tables. From the near one, he brought a chair over to the wall beside the doors, and sat down to wait as long as he had to.

In the interim, he cleaned and reloaded the pistol.

He had only to wait seventeen minutes before he heard someone outside the doors. It was the boy, he was certain, that Chin fellow, and he did not open them straight away, but held the latch in such a fashion as to signal Chuck of their presence. Meanwhile, he could hear the boy speaking with the cheerful helpfulness of wait staff everywhere, recounting the restaurant's daily specials. As the door opened, Chuck heard a gruff voice snarling, "We don't order specials, Chink."

"Of course you don't," Chin said, voice heavy with a very well-acted regret, "My apologies."

Clever kid, Chuck thought, covering his warning by playing things off as the foolishness of a yellow race. Didn't the whole restaurant play on this with its garishness and its design? Perhaps this place was not quite so awful after all.

The gruff fellow grunted some racial epithet as he entered, and declined when Chin asked about aperitifs. Chuck saw a middle sized fellow in a gray trenchcoat, with a dirty fedora atop his head and an expensive briefcase in his hand, striding toward the far table, and Chin closed the doors quickly and loudly, and the man paused to glance back.

Chuck pointed the pistol and said, "Drop the case and hands out, buddy."

The guy had a goatee, wild eyes, and a nose that showed old, poorly set breaks. "The fuck are you?"

"Nice mouth," Chuck said, "I'm not going to ask you again. Please, give me a reason to shoot you."

The case hit the floor, and then the man stood with his hands out to either side, like he was getting ready to do jumping jacks. "This wasn't part of the deal," he said. "You double crossing, pinko-commie motherfucker."

"So, I'm guessing you're not the Rose Devil?"

The man's wild eyes widened with confusion. "Fuck're you talking about?"

"What's in the case?"

"Your wife's head," the fellow said. "Or your kid's. Or your momma's. When my people get wind of this. I came here with peaceful fucking intentions—"

"And you came here to meet the Rose Devil?"

"This some kind of game? See if I squeal when a gun's pointed at me?"

Chuck said, "No games. Tell me what I want to know, or I'll kill you."

"In a crowded joint like this? That's a laugh—"

Outside, the music suddenly turned a little louder. Chin was covering any ruckuses. Chuck hid his smile. Chuck fired a round into the man's foot, and he crashed to the floor, howling.

The cries of pain from the man rolling on the floor turned into curses of the most vulgar sort.

Chuck let him vent for a while and then stood up, saying "That's more than enough."

"Fuck you, paizano. Fuck you and your family and—"

Chuck aimed the gun at the man's face. "Enough."

The man shut his mouth.

Keeping the gun on the man, Chuck approached close enough to kick the case toward his chair. Then, he backed up, sat down, and took his eyes off the man long enough to fumble with the latches. Locked.

"Combination?"

"Fuck you—"

"All I need is a reason," Chuck said. "I'll blow your brains out, your 'people' will blame the Rose Devil, and I'm sure they'll enact revenge. Works for me, since I want the Rose Devil dead, too. I might as well let your people take all the damages, spares me catching any lead." As plans went, that one was not bad. Unless someone managed to tie the whole thing back on Chuck, then it would backfire brilliantly.

"You— You're serious?"

"What do you think?"

The man considered him, still cradling his foot. "Christ, you're *serious. Who the fuck are you*?"

"Do you really expect me to say?"

"Look, buddy," the man said, "So you're after the Devil. He ain't coming here. His *people* are. Syd, the guy's name is. And Malone. And some others I didn't get their names. They sent my people an offer, and my people said 'Yeah.' I'm a fucking bagman. I don't know shit."

"Who're your people?"

"Interested parties," the fellow said.

"Paizanos?"

The guy frowned. "Yeah."

"And the paizanos are so afraid of the Devil that they're going to deal with him, instead of trying to whack him?"

"Look, buddy," the guy said, "This guy really is the fucking Devil. No one gets close to him. No one knows who the fuck he is. My people tried whacking him. They got hurt ten times as bad. It's a numbers thing. Sometimes, you gotta deal with the Devil, so's he won't burn down every fucking thing you own."

"For so long as it's profitable, huh? Sooner or later, even a Devil can make mistakes, right?"

"That's for my people to figure out. I'm just—"

"A fucking bagman. Combination?"

The guy looked into Chuck's face, and what he found there frightened him so much that he spilled the digits. As Chuck rolled the dials, he heard the door latches rattle again, heard that boy Chin outside, this time talking to someone else.

The paizano heard this too; a small amount of hope and a heavy dose of terror flashed across his face, filled his eyes. Then the doors opened. Sounds of surprise from the doorway. Maybe a dozen people, not all of them men. The paizano on the floor jabbed a finger in Chuck's direction and shouted "There's a hitter!"

Hellfire, Chuck thought, and he was up in a flash. From the doorway, he could hear the sounds of hasty hands drawing weapons, readying them to fill the room with hot lead.

Chuck blasted the nearest window. The bullet punched a hole, creating a beautiful and delicate spiderweb design, which lasted for only an instant before he jumped through. Glass cascaded around him like beautiful, cutting rain, and then he was in the garden, smelling the sweet aroma of the exotic, colorful flowers. He raced toward the wall, firing the gun blindly behind, hoping the Chin kid had enough sense to stay *down*.

The paizano bagman shouted reports of Chuck's progress, then he started pleading for mercy, ending up with the incredulous declarations "I'm just a bagman, damn it! I'm—" Three handguns roared, ending both the pleading and the pleader. Then, more handguns shredded the foliage around Chuck. He felt plenty of near misses and grazes, but nothing debilitating. Chuck tossed the case over the wall and leaped up, scrambling for natural handholds on and around the bricks.

Behind him, a squeaky voiced fellow shouted for someone, anyone to "Go get that sonofabitch!" Chuck climbed faster than he ever had before. Half a dozen handguns fired at him, and the stones exploded into chips and powder. A round zipped through his left shoulder, painting the wall with his blood. Then, a shotgun filled the air with thunder and lead. A dozen pellets stung Chuck across the left side of his back. Painful, but the round did not blow him apart. That shotgun had to be sawed off, then. Sure, a sawed off scattergun loaded with buckshot was great for close up work, could blow a man to meat in very short order. However, range allowed for a wider spread of the shot, reducing its killing potential to not-a-chance. Lucky for Chuck, the guy wasn't packing slugs.

Suddenly, a woman called for everyone to "Stop firing." Damn was her voice familiar sounding. Chuck reached the top of the wall and rolled over. As he vanished over the side, Chuck hazarded a glance back into the room.

Eight, professional looking killers stood pointing their hand cannons his way—as Chuck had expected, there were seven .45 automatics and one sawed-off, double barreled shotgun. Behind these fellows stood four others, two men, two women. The woman who was shouting for a cease fire had her arms raised in a V, and her face was—

Jesus, no.

He was seeing a ghost.

It was Selma.

Chapter Nine

Chuck hit the alley floor, mind racing like a lunatic's. *I don't believe in ghosts. I don't believe—* It couldn't be a ghost. But it couldn't be *her* could it? Selma was dead and buried. She was filling a hole in the desert . . .

Wasn't she?

His mind had to be playing tricks. He had not taken much time to look at the gunmen and their bosses, maybe with that momentary glance he had found enough similarities that his imagination could fill in the blanks. That had to be what was happening. The alternative was just too insane . . .

A man shouted for the gunmen to "Find that cocksucker! Get him back here, and bring me the case!" Had one of those men in the back, standing next to Selma—*damn it, that could not be Selma, she is* dead—looked an awful lot like Allen Lang?

A voice in his head said, *Mind tricks.* That voice sounded an awful lot like Bernie's. *Mind tricks is all this is. Focus, damn it. Focus, or you'll never make it out of this alley alive.*

Chuck grabbed the case and shoved the gun—now quite empty—into his jacket pocket. He glanced left—deeper darkness around a T-intersection, was there more alleyway, or dead ends? He glanced right, saw the bustling street. He made a decision and raced toward the bustle. As his shoe leather slapped the ground in rapid fire mode, his brain ticked along on contingencies and possibilities. Sure, they might be coming around that way, but maybe Chuck would be faster. Once he reached the mouth, there was a high probability for him to lose himself in the crowd.

Every slam of his soles against the alleyway sent vibrations of pain through his shoulder and back. He bit down on the skin of his cheek as he ran. His life, after all, depended upon this . . .

The crowd at the end was paused and looking around, aware of all those shots fired and obviously uncertain if they should be keeping an eye out for fireworks—this was a Chinese restaurant, and the average joe and jane citizen did not keep track of the Chinese festivals—or dropping where they stood, somehow seeking cover. Chuck knew his preference: *Stand around like oxen, you great stupid bastards. Confuse the enemy for me. Make it easier for me to blend and disappear.*

Like it was easier for Dexter?

Hellfire . . . Not for the first time, Chuck wondered if he was making the right decision. As the grunts of men scaling the wall behind him reached his ears, he accepted the inevitable: it's now too late to change my mind. All he could do was run and hope. Hope that he was doing the right thing and hope that the pain did not grow so great as to cloud his judgment.

He reached the end of the alley just a second too late. Behind him, the first of the gunmen's shoes hit pavement. Ahead, another of the men—this one the round-faced, almost boyish looking fellow with the sawed off shotgun—came around the side, hand in his jacket, keeping the weapon available but out of sight. Seeing Chuck, this guy grinned and pulled his hand free. Chuck's situational awareness made time itself seem to slow down, made the shotgun's emergence come at a crawl, though there remained little for him to do to prevent the weapons appearance.

A gunshot from behind punched through the meat along Chuck's left side, and Mr. Shotgun's grin vanished as he jerked and stared down at the blood spot blooming on the white shirt, about three inches above the waistline and an inch away from his tie.

Chuck found time for a grin, and he plowed into the shotgunner, knocking the fellow back. Chuck stumbled out onto the street in time for more shots fired from the wall behind him.

He screamed denials to every round that struck him, that pitched him off balance or forward, that sent him crashing to the concrete. The people on the sidewalk realized this was no foreign celebration, this was murder. They started screaming their damned heads off, running in a red hot panic. *Have to use this. Have to get away.* Chuck started crawling, though every movement filled him with uncountable agonies. *Have to—*

Someone's foot found his side, kicked once and then slid under, applied the pressure to roll him over. Onto his back. No turtle had ever felt so powerless as Chuck did in that moment, gazing up into seven barrels: two from the shotgun, the rest from .45 caliber government issue handguns. Behind all these, a blur of faces, different men to be sure but somehow the faces seemed all the same.

"Is that him?" asked a man's voice, coming closer. "Did you get that cocksucker?"

One of the blurs said "Yes we did," before two of the men parted and a new face found its way amongst them. And it was Allen Lang. No doubts, no illusions. Chuck recognized it from that video, the man who had been digging his own grave in the desert.

Chuck said, "I saw you die."

"Now I," Allen Lang grimaced before he said, "get to see you."

"Wait, Allen." That woman again, the one who looked like—

She appeared at Allen Lang's side. Chuck couldn't focus on her. He only saw her hair, long and blonde and shining in the street lights. "Not here. We have to get him away."

Allen Lang glanced back up at her. "You know this cocksucker?"

"Yep," she said. "His name is Chuck Cave."

"Uncle Chuck hisownself?" Allen Lang looked down and said, "I'll be damned."

Then the girl's face swam into focus and it was her. Selma. So pretty. The body of an eighteen year old but the eyes of someone much, much older. Like the last time he'd seen her. Like *every* time he had seen her.

"Selma," he said, but he wasn't sure she could understand him from all the blood in his mouth and throat. "You grew up."

Selma looked almost sorry when she said, "You've gotten mixed up in something rotten, Uncle Chuck."

Understatement, Chuck thought, *of the year*.

"We take him with us," she said, and Allen Lang nodded. Then, hands were under Chuck, lifting, carrying him away as somewhere nearby, but not near enough to matter, the sound of sirens wailed closer, closer, closer . . .

Even at top speed, they would arrive too late to actually do anything.

#

There is something to be said for the healing power of the dark. Even a man who has been shot to hell, who has been subjected to the worst forms of torment and torture can find a moment's surcease in the dark. In sleep. Even when nightmares threaten, when fantasies and the belches of the subconscious burble to the surface, there is relief of a kind.

The horror of the dark would come after, when the waking world itself was safe again. That was when the dark behind a man's eyelids boiled forth horrors. Until then, when the waking world offered only misery, the dark soothed.

Leaving it was the hardest thing Chuck Cave ever did, and if he had his druthers, he would have stayed. Like a boy begging for just five more minutes when mother or father is shaking him to wake for school. Just five more minutes, he may very well have mumbled, but it was already too late. The healing veil of the dark was gone and the pain returned.

"Uncle Chuck?" Was that really Selma calling him back?

He wanted to ask, *Is that really you?* but the pain said, *Your desires be damned.* Chuck could only feel the waves of weariness and agony course through him. Then, he heard the soft sound of medical equipment, the squeak of rubber gloves manipulating some sort of tubing, and then a strong artic chill froze him from the inside out, the blessed numb of morphine.

He found the strength to open his eyes, to focus on the skin tone of her face in the expressionistic wash of surreal colors. Once he found her, recognizing the qualities of her infancy, the signs of her parentage—now grown, of course—water filled his eyes. Looking upon her brought forth a second surge of morphine-like responses: chills, numbness. *Hellfire . . .*

"That better?" she asked.

He nodded, and the motion set off a hundred needle sharp points of agony in his neck and head. Throbs that quickly dulled and dimmed and then dissipated.

"Good," she said. "You know how many bullets we pulled out of you?" She did not wait long for an answer. "Seventeen. That's not counting the ones that went straight through you, either."

Though his tongue felt dry and his throat pinched shut, he found strength to say, "Selma?"

"Yeah, Uncle Chuck?"

"You're not dead?"

"Nope."

"I'm not dead?"

She laughed, not a coarse or hurtful sound merely the light sound of surprise. "Nope."

"Selma?"

"Yeah, Uncle Chuck?"

He wet his lips as he considered what to say next. Even before he had decided on a carefully worded question designed to get to the point without sounding like he was taking sides, his mouth went ahead and said what was on his mind: "My dear, what the hell are you involved in?"

Now it was her turn to fall silent. She brooded over this question for nearly a minute. On the morphine, the time dragged on and on. Finally, she broke the quiet and said, "You weren't supposed to get hurt. You weren't even supposed to be here. You . . ." She shook her head. "Why are you here, Unk?"

"What the hell," he repeated, "are you involved in?"

"Don't ask," she said. "We're going to get you well and send you home. That's the plan. If you ask too much, then you're going to spoil that plan."

"Is that the plan," he tried to clear his throat but had no success, "Allen made?"

"Allen?" she laughed, and that sound had a hardness he'd never noticed before. "He does what *I* tell him to."

He looked at her with new eyes, now. Same heart shaped face, same button nose, same hair, same old warrior's eyes, same quizzical cynical arch to the eyebrows, same figure that'd catch the boys' eyes and never let go . . . It looked like Selma next to him. She sounded the same: Same general laugh, same voice, same manner of breathing—mostly silent through her nostrils, but occasionally punctuated by a barely audible whistle inhalation through her slightly open lips—same nervous tap to her right foot. She looked the same, but this girl was a total stranger in the psychology department.

When, Chuck wondered, *did I stop knowing her? Had I ever?* Of course he had. In the graveyard, up in that tree, in a hundred other circumstances. He still knew her. The real her, just not *this* part.

"Isn't Allen the Rose Devil?" he asked.

Her laugh was little more than a turn up of the lips and a brief exhale. "Of course he is."

"Then, why would he—"

"Because I *made* him that way. Hell, Uncle Chuck, I *invented* the 'Rose Devil'."

"What? Why?"

"That's enough," she said, and something akin to compassion filled her face. "I may have said too much. Mom always called me a firebrand, and I guess my mouth doesn't know when to stop." False cheer fueled her next words: "It's good to see you, though. Have you been enjoying LA?"

"No," he said, keeping his voice steady. "I've been looking for you. Your Mother wanted—"

"Did she send you out here? Stupid cow. I called her three weeks ago, told her not to come chasing after me. I told her I'd be fine."

Chuck fell quiet, while something writhed in its death throes inside him. Was it his recollection of the girl she had been? Was it something else, pride in his ability to be a surrogate father to her, perhaps? This, of course, led to the million dollar question: *If I'd been around more, would you still have become* this *Selma? Or would you have stayed the same as the little girl I had always known? The child I had almost loved as my own . . .*

"I don't understand anything," he said.

"That's great, Uncle Chuck!" She sounded sincerely pleased at his ignorance. "You'll stay alive a lot longer that way."

"Selma?"

"Yeah?" He detected weariness in her voice, now.

"I think I'd like to be alone a while."

"All right." She stood up and sauntered toward the door. It was then that he saw she was wearing some kind of dark coveralls, a uniform. At her side was a holstered pistol, a 9mm Luger. She paused at the door, and said, "Pleasant dreams," without glancing back.

I doubt it. He said, "Thanks."

#

Chuck returned to dreams, for a time, and they proved neither pleasant nor disturbing. They were merely a means by which to pass the time, staid and stale. How long actually passed until his next visitor's arrival, he could not say. Minutes, hours, days? The world swam in and out of focus, a medicated, timeless haze. But then, the numbness began to vanish, and dull aches, pinpricks of pain, agony turned into a low, nearly subliminal buzz returned. With this came voices.

"You sure you want to turn off his morph?" This voice was a stranger's, male, boyish and whiny. The second voice, however, proved quite familiar.

"I think it's long past time for him to go cold turkey." Allen. The Rose Devil himself. "Cave, you there?" Talking like he was on a radio.

"Roger," Chuck said, and his eyes opened once, taking in Allen Lang, the all too corporeal Devil.

"Not Roger," said the Devil, "*Lang.*"

"He's still a bit loopy," said the stranger, a very young looking man in a short white coat. Was that a medical student uniform? He looked the part. A cluster of angry red acne on his cheek, freshly decanted of whiteheads. Black hair prematurely receding—the widow's peak was already noticeable—and dark eyes. Chuck figured this fellow couldn't be much older than twenty-two.

"I know you, Allen." Chuck said, "who's your friend?"

"Doc," Lang said, "say hello to Uncle Chuck Cave, Selma's godfather."

"He gonna make us an offer we can't refuse?" the medical student asked, before loudly snorting and grunting. Were those sounds supposed to be a laugh?

Chuck asked, "What do you want, Lang?"

"I want to know about you, Uncle Chuck." Lang leaned in close. "I want to know how long you can take pain. The quicker you cooperate, the sooner you get back on the sauce."

Doc said, "I though you wanted him off of—"

"Doc," Lang said, "why don't you go check on some shit next door?"

"Stick around, Doc," Chuck said, "You're bound to get a useful education. Maybe you'll finish this one."

The medical student's face turned the color of a ripe tomato, and his breaths came loud and angry. "I did finish my schooling. I'm a real doctor, you know."

"Sure," Chuck said. "My error."

"Stop dicking around with my people," Lang said, dangerous and quiet. "Dicker with me."

"What do you want from me?"

"I want to know how you got turned on to us."

"Syd sang to me. Pretty songs about Selma and you."

113

"Syd's would never squeal," Lang said, "He's going to break our old partners and then come onto our side. Why would he—"

"Syd's dead," Chuck said, showing no more emotion than if he were discussing the weather. "He tried to get me to kill Ben and Bjorn, Chloe and Emmy. When I saw through his little bullshit parade, he shot Emmy clean enough, and then we tossed him out a moving car in the desert. Dragged him a while. Then, he came clean. It was too late for him though. You ever see what all those rocks and sand can do to a man's face?"

"You're lying," Lang said, but his voice trembled as though with the terrified knowledge that Chuck was not.

"Believe as you wish," Chuck said. "I came to find Selma, I did. She's . . ."

"She's what?"

"She's dead out in that desert," Chuck said, "Syd wasn't lying about that."

"Yeah." Lang snickered. "That little girly you knew is out there all right. Got hit in the head with a rock and left for the buzzards. You ever see those motherfuckers pull at a carcass? They did that to your precious little girl. Left her bones behind to bleach in the warm, warm sunshine."

"I think I want to go home, now."

Lang glanced back at the Doc, whose complexion was ashen. "He understand anything I'm saying to him, Doc?"

"I," the medical student wet his lips, "I don't *know*. All this stuff he's saying, does he really understand anything?"

"You asking me? You're the fucking Doc. What are we paying you for?"

"Damn it, I'm a pharmacologist," the med student said. "Drugs react differently with different people. He— I—" He shook his head. "Do you think he *really* killed Syd?"

"He sure did kill that mob guy we were supposed to meet," Lang said. "The only way to square *that* with the guineas is to give them a body." When Lang looked back at Chuck, his eyes sparkled with a lunatic zeal. "And Uncle Chuck's stinking cadaver should be good enough."

"So, you won't be letting me go, huh?" Chuck asked.

"Sure we will." Lang's laugh befitted his devil moniker. Cruelty incarnate. "As far as sweet little Selma's concerned, you're going home. We're just letting the guineas take you there."

"Now I see how you sleazed your way into my goddaughter's affection." Chuck's lips found a smile. "It's been nice getting to know you, Allen Lang. I'll be seeing you soon enough."

"Oh, you're a cool one, huh? Regular ice man cometh. I tell you you're gonna die, and you just laugh at me?"

"You don't know the first thing about me," Chuck said. He could have gone on, but the little shit would not hear his words, so he left it at that. "Get out of my sight."

That was enough to set Lang off. His face went through several color transformations, from blanched white to furious red to nearly inchoate purple. "You fucking piece of—"

"Temper, temper, son," Chuck said. "And don't let the door swat your bottom. Now, if you'll excuse me, I need some healing sleep. The hot air's a bit too heavy." Chuck closed his eyes, listening to what came next while peering through the slits.

"You son of—"

Doc grabbed Lang's shoulder. "No way is he *compos mentis.* It's the morphine talking."

"Bullshit. He's . . . He's . . ." Lang stewed for a moment, and then rose quickly enough to knock his chair back a foot or two. "No more morphine for this cocksucker. I want his head clear. I want real answers before we hand him over to the wops."

He stormed out of the room, and the Doc moved to Chuck's bedside, where he completely remove the IV drop from Chuck's arm. "Sorry, pops, but it's gonna get a little painful."

That's all right, Chuck thought. *Some pain clears the head pretty quickly.*

Within the next few hours, he discovered two facts: first, he no longer needed to concentrate to keep the world in focus. Second, the Doc had lied: while it was not quite crippling, the pain that flooded his nerves was more than "a little."

Some time later, when the room was empty, he decided the time was now. He managed to sit up, to slide his feet alongside of the bed and down onto the floor, to push himself up. Stars died behind his eyelids, blinding him with excruciating supernovas. His knees buckled, dropping him to a crouch, but some mote of strength kept him from falling completely to the floor.

Slowly, he stood again, bracing himself on the steel arms alongside the bed, and then standing on his own. The pain remained, a steady nearly subliminal hum. Not so bad, after all.

Chuck ripped the tubes and medical equipment from his body, let it dangle on their lines or fall to the floor. A high pitched whine emerged from a monitor, and Chuck grinned. *Come to papa.* He sidled quickly toward the wall alongside the door.

Within seconds, he keys jangling in the knob and then the door opened. The keys brought to mind that old Jingle Bells carol. A pair of figures entered the room. "Doc" was in the lead, fumbling with a hypodermic, the cap between his teeth like a cigarette holder. Behind him came a bleached blonde nurse, curvy and about as young as the Doc.

"Myron," the nurse said, "he's gone."

Doc looked up at the bed, and the syringe cap fell out from between his teeth. "What, how?"

And Chuck struck. He closed the door with a shove, and lunged for Doc's back. Surprise gave him just enough of an advantage. He grabbed the younger man's arm and used the syringe like a knife, jabbing it into the Doc's own throat. He did not depress the plunger, however, merely held his thumb at the ready. Even if the fluid in the syringe was harmless, the needle was positioned just at that man's carotid. A simple rip and it was game over. The Doc must've realized this, as his struggles ceased once that steel tip penetrated his flesh.

The nurse's jaw dropped, and she sucked in a breath to start screaming. "Shut up or you'll both die," Chuck said. "They won't come fast enough to save you."

The nurse held her breath, shivering with fright.

"Get up on that bed," Chuck said. The nurse glanced over, but did not move. "*Now*, damn it." That prodded her, she got up onto the gurney. Chuck said, "Shut off that damn equipment." She clicked a switch and the alarm silenced. "Alright, kiddo. You're a trooper." He flashed the nurse a smile she did not return. "Talk to me Doc, where are we?"

"The compound," Doc said.

"And where is that?"

"West Hollywood. We're in a converted warehouse. There's no way you're just going to walk out of here. They've got plenty of—"

"That's my affair. Where's Allen?"

"Mr. Lang and the Dragon Lady are off site. At The Sanctum."

116

"I'm running out of patience, Doc. Tell me where they are or you're going to get a nick no styptic pencil will staunch."

"Jesus Christ, man," Doc whimpered, "They're at the Sanctum, man. The Sanctum. It's a motel he bought, a place to meditate in full view of the Hollywood sign, man." He rattled off the address, even gave driving directions. "But there's no way, man . . . No way you're gonna get there before—"

Chuck ripped the syringe out of the man's neck, and kicked him toward the bed. "I'm gonna lock you two in here. I hear you signaling the alarm, I promise you I'm coming back here and I'm gonna kill you both. Understand?"

Doc picked himself up, pouting like a baby, holding his neck. "Yeah, pops. We read you. Loud and goddamn clear." From her perch on the bed, the nurse nodded solemnly.

"Good kids," he said, and then he was out the door. A brief hallway featured four similar doors, with locks in the knobs. The hallway ended at a dead end to his left, on the other side, it opened up into a nurse's station—two chairs, a desk, a deck of cards, and plenty of paperwork filled that area—beyond that, a doorway into a large, dark space. Chuck twisted the keys, locking the Doc and the nurse in his room, removed them from the knob and smirked. He could taste freedom.

At the nurse's station, Chuck got a pretty good view of the poorly lit space beyond. Hastily erected fiberboard walls divided the nearest area into hallways and rooms. The walls only rose to roughly one story, though the warehouse itself was at least two. Above these walls, Chuck saw a steel grating floor, and through this he saw occasional figures on patrolling circuits, guards armed with automatic rifles. On both levels, irregularly spaced, hanging lights—sixty watt bulbs under steel saucer reflectors—gave a poor level of illumination to the place. Shadows ran deep. Beyond the walls, he could hear heavy machinery, forklifts and such, running constantly. The noise might be enough to cover his movements. Undoubtedly, the way out lay in that direction as well.

He searched the nurse's station for a weapon. No one had left a firearm for him, but Chuck did discover a fire ax. The blade was new and shiny. Not great, but better than being completely unarmed.

Chuck scampered out of the nurse's station and into the dim corridor, just in time for a pair of strolling guards to turn the corner on his level. They were a pair of stern faced men, similar to the professionals he had encountered in Selma's apartment building, and they had AK-47 assault rifles slung over their shoulders.

Already in the darkness, Chuck stopped moving altogether. The men were joking, taking their sweet time, and doing everything imaginable other than their jobs. Chuck silently thanked them for slouching while on duty.

One of the guards cocked a thumb at the nurse's station. "You seen Myron's new one?"

The other said, "Nuh-uh."

"A beaut. Titties out to . . ." The guard held his hands about a foot away from his chest.

"How about her hips?"

"I don't pay no goddamn attention to . . . Shit, let's stop off. I like it when she smiles at me."

"How much you pay her to do that?"

"Asshole."

They walked right past Chuck's position, and only then did he allow himself a controlled exhale. He considered continuing along the passage, but realized that would be a mistake. Soon enough, the guards' suspicions would get the better of them, and they would sound the alarm. He crept along after the men.

They stopped at the doorway to the nurse's station, muttered about her being gone. "Maybe she's in the can?" the second guy asked, and the first replied, "Wouldn't mind seeing that." The second guy made a noise of disgust.

"Yo, Darla!" the first man called. "You got visitors."

The second man cocked his head to the side, "You hear something?"

"No."

"From back there."

Both men listened, and Chuck could hear Myron's whining from the room. Was the Doc calling for help? He sounded odd, muted, then his voice stopped altogether, and the sound of a heavy weight hit the floor.

The two men glanced at each other, and started to unsling their weapons. Chuck attacked. He brought the flat of the blade around in a powerful arc, slamming it against the second man's ear. The guy squawked and dropped his weapon. His pal started to turn fully around, sputtering a curse.

Chuck drove the weapon like a spear, catching the first guard square in the bridge of the nose with the flat top edge of the blade. Cartilage snapped, the man's eyes rolled to whites, and he collapsed in a heap.

The second man was trying to call for help and fumble for the handgun at his belt. Chuck raised the ax, both hands went behind his head before he brought it down, burying the blade in the second man's chest. Steel destroyed bones and meat, and the man sputtered no more. He quickly dragged both men into the station, stashing them behind the desk before he cleaned them of weapons and ammunition. He slung the two rifles, left one pistol holstered, and then moved back toward the room.

He found the key, turned it and shoved the door open. Inside, the nurse was standing over an unconscious Doc Myron, clutching the IV Drip stand like a club. When she saw Chuck, her eyes got wide, and random syllables fell from her mouth before she found the voice to say, "He was trying to call for help. I told him to shut up. I had to hit him before he would. Please," she begged, "Please don't kill me."

Chuck glanced from the Doc to her. "Is it mostly men here?"

"Huh?"

"Guards and workers. What's the sex ratio?"

"Uhm. Almost all men."

"You want to live a little longer, right?"

"Yes."

"You know where the front door is?"

She considered this question for almost two seconds, and then she nodded.

"Then you'll help me?"

"I don't—"

"Either that or stay in here, until he wakes up. I don't think he'll appreciate what you've done very much. Help me out, and there's a chance that you'll live past tonight."

Resigned, she said, "I'll help you."

"Give me his coat."

She stripped the Doc's short white coat and tossed it to Chuck, who shrugged off the rifles and then slipped it on.

"You're a little tall," she said.

"Yeah."

"And you don't quite look like him."

"But I won't need to. We'll keep to the dark, and if we find someone, you'll be hanging on me. They won't pay me much mind. You, however, they'll look at." He waved her forward. "Of course, the arm that you'll be hanging on is the one that's got the pistol. If I get a bad feeling, like you're trying to signal for help? Guess who takes the first bullet?"

"I'll be good."

"Come here, then. Make it good."

She sidled up alongside him, hanging on his arm. This close, he could smell her perfume, a trace of vanilla and something floral. He brought the pistol up under her coat and nestled it alongside her spine. If someone was not looking too closely, they might believe he had his arm around her.

Together, they walked out the door, he locked it behind him, and they continued on through the warehouse. She whispered directions, telling him when to turn, when to keep straight. After a few minutes of wandering, they heard a second squad of guards coming along the passage. Chuck kept to the shadows, letting the lights reveal the voluptuous girl on his arm. Though it was the terror of being shot that made her bosom heave with every breath, this did not prevent the men they passed from staring at the swell of her breasts. As Chuck figured, the men only muttered a passing "hello, Doc," without actually verifying his identity.

The makeshift corridors only covered about seventy yards of ground. The rest was open warehouse space, ringed with crates and moving vehicles. Chuck said, "So this is dope central, huh?"

The nurse stared at him blankly.

"Didn't you know you were working for the leading supplier of dope for California?"

"I— *No.* I was just employed as . . ." Her eyes turned toward the floor. "I guess it makes a kind of sense. They told me they needed someone discrete, who wouldn't ask questions, who could monitor invalids. With the money they offered, it was . . . It was good. I suspected something, but . . . I needed money. I thought I could do it for a while. Wear blinders."

"Follow orders, huh? Well, you aren't the first one to be duped by a flash of green. At least you didn't sell your body, huh?"

"Yeah. At least."

"We're almost home free," Chuck said. The pain was a steady war drum, beating its tattoo on the inside of his skull. "Another two hundred yards, and there's the front door."

They made it halfway across when they heard Doc Myron's whine on loudspeakers. "Prisoner escaped, prisoner escaped. He's wearing my coat. Shoot him on sight. Repeat, shoot him on sight!"

Oh, Hellfire.

Then, the guards on the second floor started to open fire, and the crates around him burst into splinters. The dope inside sprayed through the air and across the floor. He yanked the girl behind one of the nearest crates, hopefully out of sight.

She was crying, but responsive. Chuck snapped his fingers before her eyes. "Stay with me, Darla. Focus. What do you want?"

"I want to live," she said.

"We're going to."

Another rifle opened up to Chuck's left. A three round burst stenciled the floor close to Darla's leg. Chuck came around the crate side, sighted the man through the grating above, and squeezed off two rounds in quick succession, then pulled back. He was fairly certain he saw the man topple. Another burst came from the other side. Chuck held position.

He glanced toward the door. Too far across open ground for a straight run. He cursed silently, then studied the nearby crates. Perhaps they could use them, leapfrogging from one to the next, hiding and running and hiding again. They might provide enough cover for the pair to reach the door.

If there wasn't so goddamn much light.

Chuck put a round in the lamp overhead. Then blasted two more nearby lamps, casting a full fifth of the warehouse into darkness. Now, he thought, the odds were good. He reloaded the pistol.

"We're going to run for that crate, okay?" he said, gesturing to the next nearest box in the darkness. "Don't go in a straight line. Don't slow down. Don't make yourself an easy target. You ready?"

"I—"

A guard came around the crate, rifle raised and punching holes in the box beside Chuck's head. Chuck put two in the man's face, and said, "*Go.*"

The girl ran, and five rifles opened up. She made it to safety. He was right behind her, slowed only by the four seconds it took to grab the fallen AK-47.

Boots pounded against the grating above and the floor behind the crate. As they glistened in the near darkness, Chuck could tell Darla's tears still flowed, but she was no blubbering heap. *A strong woman*, he thought.

"Ready to run again?" he asked.

"I think," she snuffed snot back into her nostrils, "I think so."

"You go that way, I'll follow after a moment."

Her head bobbed in the darkness.

"*Go.*" She went. He came around the side of the crate, rolling along the floor and staying low. Two men approached on the ground floor while three more came along the grated second story. Chuck opened up at the lower pair, sweeping the rifle along in killing arcs. The 7.65mm cartridges blew both men straight to hell. He rolled back behind cover as the men upstairs started filling the space he had been. He considered the rifle. How many rounds remained in the clip? Ten, twelve? Less?

He popped up, fired a three round burst in the area where one of the men had been. It chewed grating but not flesh. Then, he was down, again, and the men returned fire.

A new sound, then. Roaring engine coming from the right side. Chuck saw a forklift barreling toward him, its wild eyed operator leering as the steel blades surged forward.

Chuck sprayed the rest of the clip at the forklift, an attempt at suppressing fire, but none of the rounds found the operator. That dark haired man in the checkered work shirt merely sneered and gave the forklift a burst of gas.

The steel blades sheared through wood, and Chuck barely rolled aside in time to avoid being stabbed. Now, however, he was right under the vehicle, as it swerved to run him down. He kicked up slamming his boot against the vehicle's forward chassis, and then, he went for a ride. The vehicle shoved him across the cement, shredding the doctor's coat and the clothes beneath.

If that wasn't enough, Chuck heard the cacaphonhy of the blades starting to descend. The operator was trying to squash him like a cockroach.

At least the men on the second floor were no longer firing.

Chuck shoved the AK-47 into the blade tracks, jamming them in place six inches overhead. Then, he grabbed a blade, and pulled himself up and on, away from the floor. The pistol was still in his pocket, and he pulled it.

The operator's eyes showed comical shock when Chuck came around the side, and shoved the weapon into the man's face, saying "Drive for the front door."

Instead, the man dived out of the seat, onto the concrete, and rolling into the dark. Chuck let him go, sliding into the seat himself, and studying the controls. He had run similar machines at construction sites, in the long days after the army, when he was settling into Construction Contracting. Burning clutches and grinding gears was no real problem when the machine was next to disposable.

He swung the vehicle back around, heading toward Nurse Darla's crate. As he approached, he saw a guard standing over her, rifle moving up from her face toward him. He hoped the forklift would offer him the same protection it did the original operator, but readied for the worst.

Before the man could squeeze the trigger, however, Darla was up and jamming something under his chin. A syringe. Loaded with three times as much fluid as he recalled seeing in Doc's original estimation. The guard did not have time to scream, before he collapsed.

Chuck brought the forklift alongside her, held out a hand. "Want a lift?"

She took his hand, and he pulled her into the vehicle, and then gunned for the exit.

Behind him and above, automatic weapons sprayed the area, blasting his vehicle and the surrounding crates, but they were already too close to stop now. The blades slammed through the doors, and then the forklift shoved its way out, and they were free and driving through the warm, West Hollywood night.

#

When they were safe, Chuck said, "Thanks for not sticking me with the syringe."

"Yeah," she said. "I figured, if I had an opportunity, then . . . Well, I wanted to live."

"Hopefully you still do." He glanced at her, again. Not a bad looker, certainly not some dainty flower. "You be good," he said, "stay away from this crowd. Go back to school or something."

She smiled at him, then, her teeth reflecting the moonlight. "You take care, too, old fella." As he made to leave, she said, "You got a name?"

"Chuck," he said. "Chuck Cave. You?"

"Darla McCulloch."

"Good luck, Darla McCulloch."

"You're going after them? That Allen Lang and the Dragon Lady? Won't they be waiting for you?"

"I have to see this through."

"Do you?" she asked. "Why not just come away with me? We'll get out of this crazy town."

"I've made promises," he said, "and I have to follow through."

"Tough guy," she said, shaking her head with noticeable sadness.

"No," he said, "I come from a different time. One where you kept the promises you made, even if it killed you."

"I guess I'm from a whole different world," she said.

"The times and folks have changed. I'm starting to see that. But me? No. I'm still the same."

"Well, tough guy or not, you're going to need a little something to help you out." She fished a bottle out of her pocket. "This is horse strength painkillers. That guy you called Doc? He designed this."

She tossed the bottle to him. The typed label looked legit, and the contents were a pretty yellow color. They might have been packed at the local pharmacy.

"Where'd you people get these?" he asked.

"Take one to make the pain go away," she said. "Afterward you won't be driving any forklifts, though."

He dry swallowed one pill. It stuck in his throat, making him force it down. The psychosomatic response told him he was feeling better. The pill could have been sugar for all he knew. "How many can I take a day?"

"Well, as many as you want," she quipped. "I'd stick to one every twelve hours if you want to keep doing things. Like breathing."

"Thanks, McCulloch."

Her face softened, and her eyes shimmered with the tears of someone stuck on the edge of complete uncertainty. Until this moment, she'd had a life and knowledge about where tomorrow would take her. What she would do this week, this weekend, next month . . .

All that was over now, and Chuck could see the knowledge settling into her bones. The knowledge and the horror that came with it. Still, she managed to find heart when she said "You're welcome, Cave."

Then, he turned around and walked away. To The Sanctum.

Chapter Ten

The Sanctum Motel turned out to be a U-shaped structure of connected bungalows, nestled in the hills, with a none-too-bad view of the infamous letters spelling out the pinnacle of plenty of folks' dreams. The bungalows were in good shape, and the sign for the place—which bent the name Sanctum around the C, and used the Motel part to form a triangle—blared out life and presence with authority, brighter than the stars in the sky. Blue neon underneath brazenly announced No Vacancy.

Chuck might have been expecting something a bit less showy, a bit more restrained. Perhaps even something that was a rundown wreck. No dice, this place had all the glitz of Vegas, and so few cars that the illusion of No Vacancy could come under question if proper scrutiny were placed. The cab driver pulled past before Chuck said, "Stop anywhere up in here."

"You sure, pal?"

"Yeah." Chuck held up a twenty. "And Mr. Jackson here agrees with me."

Not one to turn down a nice tip, the cab driver pulled over. "You need me to wait?"

"Nope," Chuck said, "but you might want to call the cops."

"Cops, why?"

"I think there's going to be trouble up here."

"Hey, pal. I don't want no part of trouble."

"The only part you have," Chuck said, "is bringing trouble to their door. Call the cops if you want, but that's just gravy. You're done and can go home." Chuck got out and paused when McCulloch's horse-strength painkiller set his vision swimming. He thought he might be blacking out.

When the sensations passed enough for him to operate, Chuck closed the door quietly behind him. He pulled the pistol out and checked the clip—one full magazine in the weapon, one three quarters full in his pocket—and the cab's tires screeched against the pavement. Soon, the vehicle's rear lights faded into the dark.

Dawn was still a few hours off, and the moon had set, but with that sign, the Sanctum Motel was brighter than Jesus. Chuck tucked the pistol in his pocket, and sauntered up the road, keeping his head down, but nevertheless studying the surroundings. Soon enough, he saw sentries in the trees and underbrush. Men with rifles and scopes trained on him. Nice.

He could hear Bernie in his head, "Hope you know what you're doing, boss."

"So," he whispered to himself, "do I." He kept his hands steady at his sides, and walked all the way back to the Motel, then into the central courtyard parking lot, and over to the building marked "Office".

A slender fellow with tussled chestnut colored hair sat behind the desk. He wore a stained undershirt and a pair of welder's goggles around his neck. He did not glance up when he said, "We's all filled up."

On the wall behind the counter, a rack of keys hung next to a playboy centerfold. The latter had been made family friendly through the judicious use of a black pen. The former had half its keys on display. Decidedly familiar looking keys. They were carbon copies of the ones in Selma's secret stash spot. Of course, the baggie was gone, now. Taken from him around the time he had been delivered to the clinic.

Chuck said, "Didn't see many cars out there."

Now the fellow stopped staring at his newspaper, giving Chuck an irritated glare. "We's full up, anyway."

In the distance, Chuck heard sirens approaching. Still too far off for him to tell if they were coming here. He hoped the hack driver had done the smart thing, radioed in a call for the cops. He hoped the dispatcher would receive and act properly on the message. "I don't want a room, anyway."

"Oh, what d'ya want, then?"

"A guy named Lang. Tell me what room he's in?"

The guy's irritation vanished and raw nerve anxiety filled in the emotional vacuum. "Lang, you say?"

"Allen Lang," Chuck replied, "though he might be booked under Devil-comma-Rose."

Now the guy moved. He brought up a sawed-off, double-barreled, twelve gauge shotgun, and Chuck dove behind a nearby couch as the barrels coughed and filled the air with a spreading mist of deadly buckshot. Cushions exploded, filling the air with fluff. The couch's springs burst out the front side with audible twangs. Very little of the shot actually penetrated, and for that Chuck was grateful.

After letting the shotgun bark, the man started to drop behind his counter, hoping the wooden structure might offer him equivalent cover that the flower patterned couch with the steel frame offered Chuck. Unfortunately for him, Chuck already had his pistol ready and he had put two rounds in the man's chest before his weight hit the floor.

"Talk to me," Chuck said. "Where is he? Talk and I'll let you live."

"Fuck you," was the man's only response. Accompanying this, the pounding footfalls of more men coming in fast as stampeding cattle.

Behind Chuck was a plate glass picture window. Beside that a storm door. Too many vantage points. He was up and rushing for the counter. Leaping up onto it and rolling across and behind just before the Rose Devil's men arrived and started filling the area with lead.

Chuck landed on the slender man but felt no guilt for causing him more pain. He landed just in time to disrupt the man's reloading his scattergun. Not that it would serve him well. The first of Chuck's rounds had punched into the guy's right shoulder. Aiming would be a nightmare, since that was the shoulder that controlled his gun hand.

"Give," Chuck said and pulled the shotgun out of the slender man's hands. He popped the two fresh rounds in and sealed the breach. Shotgun in left hand, pistol in right, Chuck waited for a pause in the weapons fire. When it came, he rose up enough to see the shadows of men outside, reloading from their positions around the door. One of the gunsels proved to have a skill at speedy reloading, and he came around the doorway first, gun poised to raise some Hell. A familiar face, this was one of the men who had come after him at the restaurant.

Chuck shot him as he came around, and the round punched through the man's cheek. The man's finger twitched on the trigger, and the weapon sent fully automatic death across the other side of the doorway, ripping through one of his companions—through the legs, if the screaming could be believed. The man Chuck shot dropped and clawed at his face.

A shadow across the picture window signaled someone taking too far a step backwards. Chuck hit one of the shotgun's triggers and blew out the glass, followed this up with a 9mm slug.

Suddenly hot pain jabbed into Chuck's ankle. He looked down, saw the hotel desk man had stabbed him with what appeared to be a decorative letter opener. Chuck introduced a 9mm cartridge to the man's heart, before collapsing behind the wood.

Outside, someone stage whispered, "Who is this guy?" and another voice said, "Dunno."

"I'm here for the Rose Devil," Chuck said. "Got no beef with you people. You hear those sirens? They're coming here. Someone want to tell me where Lang is?"

Silence. Ah well, it was worth a try. Chuck found several holes in the counter, large enough to see what was going on in the foyer and near the front door. Neither of the gunsels was stupid enough to try and rush him, but their shadows were anxious enough. Jerkily moving, caught between loyalty and the flight instinct.

"What's the room number—"

"Fuck you," the gunsel with the blasted face shouted, "Fuck you, fuck you!"

Fine, Chuck thought. I'll do this the hard way.

Chuck leaned over the counter long enough to put a round in his brainbox, and the profanity ceased. Then, he dropped back down again. A cursory glance found an open box of shotgun shells. Nice. He pocketed a few, and broke open the breach of the weapon, removed the spent rounds and replaced them.

Then, someone came running into the room.

Chuck popped back up to find a man wearing a trim moustache and a rumpled leisure suit carrying two revolvers, rushing toward a side doorway—a kitchenette, from the poor position Chuck had. The man cut loose, but trying to run whilst firing two handed was his downfall. The rounds missed Chuck by miles, but Chuck's shotgun did not. The man fell forward, squealing as his blood and guts drizzled onto the floor like a summer storm. As he dropped behind cover, once more, one of the men at the doorway opened up with his assault rifle. Splinters and lead cut grooves across Chuck's cheeks, punched through his side. Breathing grew difficult and every inhale he took made an awful sucking sound.

That was bad.

Chuck brought the shotgun up toward the room's rear window, and fired the last barrel. Glass exploded, and then he was up again, putting his foot on the counter and shoving off. Hitting the window and breaking through, into the grassy lot behind. A startled man tried to shoot him, but Chuck fired his last two rounds, scoring one hit. The gunman dropped into the grass, wailing and clutching his groin. Chuck rushed over, scooped up the man's .30-06 hunting rifle, and ducked into the overgrowth to reload his weapons.

Not many rounds left . . .

Time to move. Rising, his vision swam. Still, he rushed parallel to the buildings. Behind, he heard the sounds of pursuit. Of course, he was on the enemy's territory, no way would they let him past their 5 yard line without a fight.

Thankfully, the sirens were getting louder, and that was leading to a whole other source of chaos. Some of the enemy was trying to get away, the rest . . .

Chuck glanced up to the nearest roof. Now that would be the catbird seat, wouldn't it? He gritted his teeth in a grin.

No way would Lang sit around waiting for Johnny Law to show up. He'd be trying to make good his own escape. Dark as it was back here, Chuck was not sure how much time he might have to get to the wall and climb. Could he make it before the pursuers showed up?

It was a question of hope. He had little other choice. Running through the brush was just going to wear on him faster. He hocked a loogie into the brush, trying not to notice how much blood taste was in amongst the phlegm.

He hurried toward the nearest wall, used a window to pull himself up. Found another handhold. Yanked. Felt his insides turn to lava, bit back the scream.

Weapons fired, the cartridges chewed through the wall, one zinged past his already wounded leg. Determination along carried

Chuck up and over, and he lay there, panting on the roof, waiting for the world to stop being so confused.

Below he heard two men arrive, also panting, and arguing as to who should or would climb up after him. Chuck ended this argument with both barrels from the shotgun. Then, despite what his body was telling him, he rose again and scampered across the roof, toward the courtyard side. He did not cross all the way, merely paused at the arch of the roof, to observe.

Oh yes, the lights were coming closer, along Mullholland, and the sirens, like the wild cries of beautiful birds on the hunt, approached. Men were running like crazy, trying to get to the few vehicles.

From one of the rooms, Lang and Selma rushed toward a white van. Lang carried a pair of attaché cases, while Selma carried a rifle. Thick as thieves, those two.

Chuck braced his .30-06 and sited for the running Lang. His round blew out Lang's hip when that man was not twenty feet from the van. Lang sucked air, hit the ground and called Selma's name. She stopped running, returned to Lang's side and grabbed one of the cases, before once more rushing for the van.

By then, Chuck had put another round into the chamber and was following her progress with the rifle. He had her in his sights, dead to rights, and he heard Bernie in his head saying, "Take the shot," but his finger remained frozen over the trigger.

Then she arrived at the vehicle's sliding side door and hurried inside, out of sight.

Chuck changed targets. He put one round through the driver's side of the windshield, and was rewarded with the vehicle swerving wildly. This gave him enough time to expel the spent shell and lever in a new one. This cartridge he put into the engine block, and the van shut down as sweet as could be.

Selma bolted from the van, rushing back to the room she and Lang had come from. She was bloody faced, banged up from the van's demise, but still running strong. The Devil lay in the dirt, groaning for her to "Help me, damn you! Help me!"

Chuck walked up, going slow. Though the painkillers he had taken were keeping the pain at bay, they were playing serious hell with his head. Or was that the bloodloss from getting shot at again?

Lang heard his shoes on the gravel and dirt. Rolled to see Chuck's face, and purest hatred transformed the downed man into a damn near literal devil. "You stinking cocksucker! I should've killed you outside Manchurian Smoke!"

Chuck waved the rifle barrel before the Devil's eyes. "Probably," he said. "Then you wouldn't be here, would you?"

"You going to kill me? You going to squeeze that trigger? Do it, old man. Fucking do it."

"You talk so much shit," Chuck said.

"I'm the fucking now, man! I'm the future, too—"

Chuck shoved the rifle barrel into Allen Lang's gob and that broke the bravado. The Devil was crying, now. A terrified child. This was the future. "Your words are poison, Allen. Your ideas are shit. You ruin people, and you don't think retribution is coming. Well, I'm here to say that it is, Allen. People like you are not untouchable, not at all. Because there are people like me." Chuck curled his finger on the trigger. "Goodbye, Allen Lang," said Chuck, and the rifle said, *click*. Empty. "Ooops," Chuck said, not at all surprised.

Allen's ire was coming back, but the man's groin was wet, his eyes were leaking tears. Chuck kicked him in the shattered hip, and Allen reeled in pain for a moment before he dropped into unconsciousness.

Chuck staggered forward. Toward Selma's room. He swung the door open and found Selma inside, a gun pointing toward the door. It was a semi-automatic handgun, small caliber. Maybe a .22 Llama. Chuck couldn't say for certain—all that mattered was it was a gun whose business end was pointing at him.

His eyes and attention were fixed on the girl pointing it. Her hand was shaking, her face a mess of grief. *Maybe a little guilt*, Chuck thought, *or is she beyond all that?*

Suddenly, he recalled the name of some philosopher's book, one the Nazis had proselytized from. The title was *Beyond Good and Evil* though the author was lost to time and Chuck's memory. The title was enough, though. Looking at the little girl he had known he saw that she had become everything that title was trying to communicate. *When*, he wondered, *had Selma become a nihilist's wet dream?*

"You going to shoot me too, kiddo?"

He waited for her answer, standing in the door, rifle at his side. Finally, she looked away, furious and terrified. "God damn it, Uncle Chuck." Her gun lowered.

"Is this it?" he asked, indicating the space around them with a shrug of his shoulders. "The room for the keys?"

"What are you talking about?"

"The keys I found in your hidey hole."

She shook her head, blank as to what he was saying.

"In your old apartment. Under the slats. You had a manifesto and a baggie of keys. And now you aren't even listening to me."

He looked around the space. It was a packing room. Scales and baggies and tables. Some cocaine. *The other key from that baggie.*

On the wall was an open safe. A few stacks of bound green in there, a single packet of white powder, leaking its contents through an accidental rend.

He nodded to himself. "Yeah, I think this must've been the room."

Finally she emerged from whatever thoughts she had been struggling with. Emerged to snap "What are you talking about?"

She was no trapdoor spider. There was nothing fearsome to her. Not now.

I'm talking about answers, damn you. I'm talking about rationales and reasons and that stupid little baggie was supposed to be the key to making sense from it all. I need answers.

Then, he wondered if he needed them at all. Life had not handed out all that many so far. Why did he expect it to now?

"It doesn't matter," he said, unable to keep the bitterness at bay any longer. "Nothing matters but that the cops are coming. You and Allen are finished."

Her gun hit the floor, and she cried into her hands. "He made me, Uncle Chuck. He—"

"Don't you dare do that," he said. "You know what you did. Take responsibility for Christ's sake."

Her hands dropped away. The tears still dripped down her cheeks, but the faux grief was gone. The little girl she had been was gone, too. There was nothing left. This woman was a cipher, a complete empty place. "You know what?"

"No, but I bet you're going to tell me."

She wiped the back of her hand across her eyes. The crocodile tears vanished like so much sweat. "You sound just like my mother."

He considered this and then shrugged. "There are worse people to imitate."

Selma shook her head, stone cold and hollow-eyed. "She's walking dead, Unk. And I'm alive. I was free."

"Maybe you were," he said. "For a little while, maybe. But tell me: What are you now?"

Selma said nothing. She rocked in place, thinking and stewing and planning. *A hell of a thing to see*, Chuck thought, *her sitting there like a little psychotic.*

Then, the police arrived, sirens wailing and lights flashing. Just in time. Chuck could no longer hold the rifle. He could only let it fall, and slumped in the doorframe, hoping that someone would find him before it was too late. Would take her away before she got her ideas straight. Would take her away before her ideas could infect him like a flu virus.

After that, the soothing darkness called him home, and there were no dreams. Only moments of peace and freedom from pain.

#

Consciousness arrived in snatches: a few seconds stolen here, a few there. He heard dozens of voices, many spoke directly to him, asking questions that made no sense, but most were directed to those around him. He saw folks in white uniforms, and stern faced folks in blue ones, and eager faced folks in suits with notepads and cameras, and a sweet faced, blonde haired girl smiling at him and it was Selma, no, not Selma, it was Chloe, and she was telling him, "Rest now, daddy-oh, and heal.

"The war is over."

#

That was wishful thinking, of course.

In time, he did heal. In time, he returned to the world of the conscious. It was far too late to be a part of things, however. The words associated with his case were "indefinitely comatose" and by the time he was once more among the living and aware, nearly a year had passed and most of the fighting was done.

He had to play catch up.

Many papers referred to the events at the Sanctum Motel as "The Urban War to End All Wars" and it called Chuck a hero, a fatherly figure out to rescue his goddaughter and put an end to one of the biggest dope smuggling rings on the West Coast. Other news agencies painted him as a no good vigilante, making him almost as reprehensible as the men he was fighting.

The evidence was strong enough to put Lang away for life without possibility of parole. Not a week after he'd gone inside, however, one of the incarcerated "guineas" he had been so vocally opposed to shanked him in the showers.

Selma proved to be a crafty one. All along, she had slanted the evidence, predetermined the path the police would take and made Lang completely responsible. By the time different evidence came to light, she had already plea-bargained her situation down to misdemeanors and served out her hours of community service. After that, she was on a plane to Europe. All without bothering to once speak to her mother.

Bernie was already back in Massachusetts by the time Chuck came around. His eye could not be salvaged, and the brain damage he suffered was minor, but he only took the first of Chuck's phone calls, offering a cryptic, "I need time to heal, man. I'll be calling you again some day. Soon, maybe."

Chuck had said, "So far as I'm concerned, we're even Bernie."

"We're anything but," Bernie had said. "Now, you owe me one. A grand whopper of one, too. An eye's worth." After that, he did not take or respond to Chuck's phone calls. After a while, Chuck stopped trying.

Ben and Bjorn disappeared into the criminal underground, tried to remake themselves into hoods, and failed miserably at it. A week before Chuck woke up, Bjorn washed up on a beach, and Ben found his way into prison.

That left Chloe . . . She managed to avoid involvement with the police. She escaped incarceration by acting as a witness for the prosecution and helped put Lang away. For the first five months, Chloe had sat at Chuck's bedside, talking to him, trying to woo him back from the land of the living dead. After that, she stopped coming all together. Had she lost interest? Had her past caught up with her? Chuck had no way to contact her, no way to know for sure. He silently wished her well, hoping for the best, but rowing for shore . . .

#

The system prosecuted Chuck for assault, assault with a deadly weapon, vigilantism, illegal discharge of a firearm, and manslaughter. The court trial lasted thirteen days. In the end, the jury found Chuck not guilty on the counts of manslaughter, vigilantism, and illegal discharge; they found him guilty for the assault and assault with a deadly weapon charges. According to the California State Penal Code, Chuck Cave received a hefty fine and one hundred seventy hours of community service. Combined with the year he had spent in a hospital and the subsequent two years of physical therapy, his life was pretty well ruined by the time he was ready to return to New York. He considered staying out in California for a while, maybe retiring properly. But California was not home.

He had a stop to make before he could rest, anyway.

Epilogue

Like most small towns across these United States, Drucker's Meadow Pennsylvania was not prone to radical changes all too quickly. Though the year was now 1978, the town itself looked pretty much like it did twenty years earlier. A town hall dominated the central square, and colorfully named shops with equally colorful awnings (many cloth, several plastic) filled most of the streets of the downtown area. The houses, radiating from this central section, were spacious and set on nice sized lots of land. Sons and daughters shoved lawn mowers with the same levels of irritation that they always had, and for the families without kids, the fathers were out there, smoking and pushing and wondering how the Steelers were doing.

The Kowalski house was little changed from the last time Chuck had visited it. A colonial style home with large bay windows, and a carefully groomed lawn. Cheerful looking flowers and small bushes alongside the porch. The cane he was using was black and heavy with a walnut, pistol-grip handle. The tip was shod with rubber, and this made a solid tick-tock with every step he took.

When he rang the bell, Bea Kowalski did not answer. Instead, a young, black woman in a blue dress did. She glanced at his cane first, considering the threat it posed. Wariness clung to her voice when she asked, "Can I help you?"

"Is Bea Kowalski here?"

The woman glanced over her shoulder in that nervous instinct some folks have to give away answers they would prefer to keep secret. "May I ask who is calling?"

"My name is Cave. Chuck Cave. I was a friend of—"

"Oh yes. *Yes.* I know all about you." Peace settled across her face, then. A hint of a relieved smile. "Won't you come in?"

As he entered, Chuck said, "I think you have me at a disadvantage."

"Marietta James," she said, "I'm Ms. Kowalski's nurse."

137

"Her nurse?"

"She has, well, her spells every now and again. I'm live in help. I clean up, make the food, take care of her when she needs me to. If you'll have a seat over here in the living room, I'll see if Ms. Kowalski is up for visitors just now."

Chuck walked into the living room, and discovered that it was not so well named. The room was anything but lived in. Occupied with things, certainly, but while the carpet was vacuumed and clean, the room stank of disuse. He found his way to the chocolate brown sofa, now covered with a dust guard, and sat down. The transparent plastic squeaked and squawked underneath him, sending up fresh complaints with every shift or twist.

Marietta returned after two minutes. "She's come right around when I told her you were here. We'll give her a moment to ready herself, though." Marietta sat down and started to talk, asking questions about Los Angeles, about how long he was planning on staying around Drucker's Meadow, the typical chit chat that folks west of the Hudson and across the Great Plains prided themselves on sharing. She was amiable enough and a good listener. As well, she had stories aplenty herself, some amusing, some touching, some tragic, about people Chuck had never met.

After a few of these, Bea made her appearance, sweeping into the room like some southern matron, all a titter. Chuck stood up and smiled, but the first thing he thought was, *When did you start looking so* old. Shame turned his eyes down to the floor.

The years had not been kind. Bea's hair was now almost solid white and matted. Her face and hands were messes of wrinkled, withered flesh, spotted with age and tobacco. She had applied her makeup with a trowel, in rich colors that emphasized how washed out her complexion really was.

"Charles," she said, "so nice, so *good* to see you."

"Hello, Bea."

"Always so dapper, just like you stepped off a movie screen fresh from a scene with Dean Martin or that Frank Sinatra." She came to him, and held his shoulders, while bending forward to kiss the air on either side of his face, and then leaned back again. "Travelling again?"

He nodded.

"And where are you off to this time?"

"Home," he said.

"Ah yes, of course. From . . .?"

"California."

"Mr. Cave been in Los Angeles," Marietta said.

"Have you seen Selma?" Bea asked. "How is she doing?"

Chuck did not know what to say. He stood in awkward silence, feeling his face contort in a confused paroxysm of stupification and false cheer.

"Mr. Cave said she was doing good, last time he saw her," Marietta said, speaking slow and loud, as one might to the hard of hearing. Her voice returned to normal when she asked, "Didn't you, Mr. Cave?"

"Right."

"She calls me regularly," Bea said. "But I haven't *seen* her in, Lord, so long. One of these days, I should fly West. Fly out and see my sweetie. She's looking good you say?"

"Yes," Chuck said. He tapped the cane against the floor, and Bea did not seem to notice it at all.

"Wonderful, wonderful. Thank you Chuck. You saved her, I know you did. From that man. That awful, awful man. And now she's free to go to school and break hearts and meet a rich boy. A nice boy. A wholesome and religious boy. Has she?"

Chuck floundered for an answer before settling on, "Not, uh, yet."

Bea continued, non-plussed. "In time, in time. These things are preordained, I'd say. Only a matter of time before they come to pass. And when she's ready to settle down with her nice, wholesome boy, then I'm sure she'll invite me out. Or maybe they will come here, come home. For the wedding, yes. The wedding. And it will be beautiful, chiffon and taffeta . . ." Although she was blinking, this was not helping her come back from whatever place she was in now. Whatever dark, peaceful place she decided was to be her own mental home.

"Beautiful," Chuck said, but a lump in his throat made the word little more than a croak.

"And of course," Bea continued, "she wouldn't forget you. Not her favorite Uncle Chuck. Not the man who saved her life."

"Of course not," Chuck said.

They sat together, Bea talking and Marietta agreeing and Chuck playing along, for almost an hour. Then, it was time for Bea to get some rest, and time for Chuck to go.

Marietta led Bea away, before seeing Chuck to the door.

"Does Selma really call?"

Marietta shook her head. "My little one does. Well, she's not so little now. Living in Pittsburgh and got a husband and little one of her own. She calls every month regular, though. Plays the part. Says everything to make Bea happy. That's all we can do, you see."

Chuck nodded. "We do what we can, yeah." Marietta nodded sagely, and then she closed the door, and Chuck stood on the porch, staring at the walls, at the lawn, at the garden beside the porch, marveling at how, on the outside anyway, it looked no different than it had for the last twenty years. Wondering what in the hell he was supposed to do now.

He walked, as well as he could. He could move without the cane, but he liked having the weight in his hand. His feet led him to the road and back to town. A car would be waiting to take him to the airport, to take him home. He had never felt more ready to lie down for a lifetime and sleep.

Acknowledgements

This novel would not have been written without help from quite a few people. The author is indebted to each and every one of them for their tiny (and often unknowning) contributions to my sanity and creativity.

First up, thanks have to go out to Carlos Dunn. This novel would not exist without him. How's that? Well, I wrote the first Chuck Cave story for him. All of them, really. Although I wrote this novel for myself, the book came out of that work, and while it's not something that fits his publishing paradigm, these days, I hope it's one he can enjoy.

Lucy A. Snyder and Gary A. Braunbeck have been supportive writers and even better friends. They are, in short, some really fine folks. Supportive and encouraging and downright wonderful folks. I owe them more than I can ever repay, and I highly endorse their books. You can't go wrong with a Snyder urban fantasy or a Braunbeck nightmare story.

Jerry Gordon, Maurice Broaddus, the dearly missed Sarah Larson, and all the Indiana Horror Writers have been some fine folks to get to know. As are Jack Haringa, Christopher Golden, and all the members of the New England Horror Writers. As are Lee Thomas, Wrath James White, and all the members of the Heart of Texas Horror group. Wow, I belong to a lot of regional horror groups.

Also many thanks to all the attendees at Mo*Con and NECON for making me feel welcome and, yes, loved.

Of course, mucho kudos to my folks, Jan and Dan, who have been supportive of my crazy writing ideas for years. Here's one I'm pretty pleased with. Couldn't have done it without you!

And of course, this novel would not exist without the tireless endeavors of one person: my wife, Trista. She's been with me through the thick and the thin, and she has never let her enthusiasm for my (sometimes unpaying) career wear thin. I was a lesser man without you, honeybunny. I love you dearly, and I'm grateful to have you in my life.

If you enjoyed this Book,
be sure to look for these other works
by C. C. Blake:

Cave's Urban Fantasy Thrillers
Cave and the Vamp (Cave and the Vamp pt. 1)
Cave and the Feral Angel (Cave and the Vamp pt. 2)
Hell on Earth (Cave and the Vamp pt. 3)
Cave's Dark Mistress (Cave and the Vamp Side Trek)
Cave's Deadly Beauties (Cave and the Vamp Side Trek)

The Valkyrie Force Post-Zombpocalypse Series
Kane and the Hungry Dead (Valkyrie Force #1)

Dark Fantasy Adventures
Bloody Business: Thrilling Tales of Undead Danger
Confess, Witch: Thrilling Tales of Occult Danger
Countdown on Hex Island (with Kaysee Renee Robichaud)
Divinest Sense
The Murder Cage
Mystic Dangers: Thrilling Tales of Supernatural Adventure
Nightmare Stories
The Sacrifice

Science Fiction Adventures
The Positronic Pretty: Rick Cave Space Opera Adventure #1
The Beauty Snatchers: Rick Cave Science Fiction Adventure #2
NAStar Driver (Vol. 1): Two Laps Around the Space Lanes
To Honor Her Father: A Science Fiction Revenge Story

Suspense Thrillers
The Ballad of the Cop's Gun
Chuck Cave and the Vanishing Vixen
Dark
Dirty
Fatal Femmes: Sexy Spy Adventures
Five Crimes
The Go-To Girl
In the Clutches of El Diablo: Sexy Suspense Adventures
Nine Thrillers

Seller's Market
Trapped Like Rats
Wayne and Bean

About the Author

C.C. Blake has lived across the United States, starting in the suburbs of Detroit, to Massachusetts' second largest city (Worcester) to the country's seventh largest city (San Antonio, Texas, that is). He's has a variety of jobs, working as a substitute teacher, the graveyard shift dishwasher at a haunted Denny's, lab research monkey and teaching assistant at a second tier college. Currently, he works as an automation consultant for a chemical company on the Northeast side of SAtown (which isn't as Hellish as it sounds).

Blake's most popular character, irrepressible adventurer Chuck Cave, has appeared in over two dozen stories, including the 2005 *Man's Story 2* Story of the Year Award winner "Chuck Cave and the Vanishing Vixen."

In addition to his pulp stories for the 2-Empire (*Man's Story 2, Vampires 2, Androids 2* and *Paranormal Romance 2*), Blake's fiction has appeared in several anthologies, including *Unparalleled Journeys II* (from Journey Books Publishing) and *Fearology: Terrifying Tales of Phobias* (from Library of Horror Press).